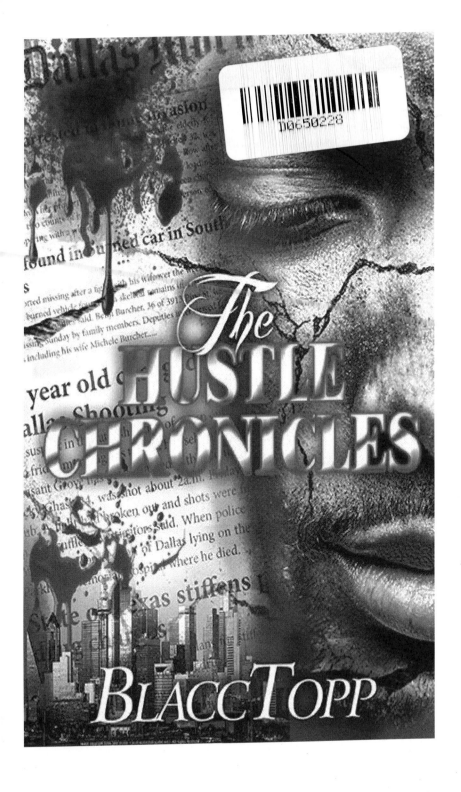

The HUSTLE CHRONICLES

BLACCTOPP

The Hustle Chronicles®

The Hustle Chronicles

Is a work of fiction. Any resemblances to real people living or dead, actual events, establishments, organizations, or locales are intended to give the fiction a sense of reality and authenticity. Other names, characters, places and incidents are either products of the author's imagination or are used fictitiously. Those fictionalized events & incidents that involve real persons did not occur and/or may be set in the future.

Published by:

BlaccStarr Media Group
Written by: BlaccTopp
Inside Layout: Linda Williams
Edited by: Dolly Lopez/Linda Williams
Cover design by: www.mariondesigns.com

ISBN: 978-1-62209-371-7

For information contact:

BlaccStarr Media Group
P.O. Box 9451
Port St. Lucie, FL 34985-9451

blaccstarrmg@gmail.com
www.facebook.com/mrblacctopp
twitter...@mrblacctopp
instagram....blacctopp

Dedication

This book is dedicated to the ones that I have lost that were near and dear to me: Naje' Brashford, my beautiful mother; my daddy, Rufus Swift Jr.; my two sisters Reba Victoria, and Anna Catherine. My uncle Rabbit, and my step dad Mervie "Booty" Green. R.I.P to each of you. I miss you more than you will ever know. See you at the crossroads!!!!

Always,
Mr. BlaccTopp

Acknowledgements

First and foremost, I would like to thank the Almighty for all of the blessings that He has bestowed on me. I would like to thank my father (R.I.P.) for my tenacity and drive. I would like to thank my mother (R.I.P) for my artistic nature and my educational fortitude. Thank you to my extended family The Swearinger's, who raised me along with their two children Ray and Tranika and treated me as their own instead of letting the streets have me. Thank you to my little brother Devon and his wife, Miranda (my Panda) for always keeping it 100 even when I didn't want to hear it.

To my brother Royce, thank you for being a constant source of support and unbridled enthusiasm. Love you much, Playa! And to Linda and Dolly, thank you for seeing my vision and helping to bring these pages to life!!

To my literary family: Treasure Blue, Kisha Green, and Asia M. Butler. Regardless of whether you guys know it or not, I draw constant inspiration from your grind and determination, not to mention y'all write some bomb ass books!!! WRITE ON!! Shout-out to Unique and Cheryl Melvin, Hakim from Black And Nobel Book Store and Extreme John Bermudez, thanks for all the love and believing in me.

To Kalil, my only son, Kalani, my little Noodle Booty, and my last pea out of the pod, Kailyse. My life belongs to you three, no questions asked. I love you with every ounce of breath in my body. Never let boundaries keep you from reaching your goals. A dream is only reality yet to be revealed. Dream big my, babies! Dream big!!

To my gorgeous wife, I love you, baby girl thank you. Thank you, thank you, for understanding my eclectic literary nature. For putting up with my mood swings and for being my biggest fan and a beacon of hope when I not only doubted my talents, but when I doubted us. I am forever indebted to you. To all of you that I consider my friends, thank you.

Prologue

My Brother's Keeper

Julius Gage had three brothers, Otha Lee, Eugene and Charles. They had come up in the country life of deep woods Arkansas. Julius and Charles were the closest of all of the siblings. He was the oldest of the four boys, and Charles was the youngest. Wherever Julius went, Charles went and Julius didn't mind one bit.

It was Charles who had discovered their mother's body and had run nonstop to the barn to find Julius. Their father had killed their mother in a fit of rage.

Gertrude Gage was a full blooded Choctaw Indian, and she was as beautiful as the day was long. She worked for the rich and well to do white folks in Marianna Arkansas; a job that she neither loved nor hated. It was a means to an end.

Julius' mother was walking home from a long hard day of cleaning toilets and taking verbal abuse from her white employers when it had begun to rain. It was a heavy constant downpour so she had taken shelter in an abandoned warehouse on the long country dirt road that led to her family's farm. Although she decided that she would wait there until the rain subsided, she knew her husband would be angry because she would be late getting home to cook dinner. But if she walked all the way home in the rain she would surely catch her death of cold.

The rain beat a rhythmic pattern of trebles and basses on the roof of the old warehouse. As Gertrude stood in the doorway of the building looking out at the rain she thought of how dramatically her life had changed, and not for the better. She had endured many years of torture and beatings at the hands of the man that she called her husband.

Nathaniel Gage was a mean man. He was very hard to deal with and even harder to live with but, they were married, and in her mind once you were married it was until death.

Enough was enough though, and she decided that maybe she should just take her boys and move back to the Reservation. At least there she would have the support of her family. She had disobeyed her father's wishes by marrying Nathaniel, but he had promised her the world, with his light features and syrupy tongue. She had fallen for it hook, line and sinker.

Now as she looked out into the dark sky her world felt as though it was crashing down around her. How could he beat her so mercilessly if he loved her? Nate would beat her for breathing too loud. Gertrude was beaten for any small infraction, and it was getting old. Each time he beat her he would apologize, only to beat her again. She felt like every time he put his hands on her he took a little bit more life from her. A once gorgeous woman with a glowing smile had now become a pretty face with a faded smirk. The memories of how Nate had once treated her lit the corners of her mind like candles. It gave her a mix of emotions. She was angry with her husband for treating her as if she didn't matter, but she was still deeply in love with him. She wanted to leave, but she knew that he and the boys needed her.

The rain was beginning to lift and had settled into a light drizzle so Gertrude picked up her bag and exited the warehouse, knowing full well that there would be hell to pay when she got home if she couldn't make Nate understand how the rain had put her behind schedule. She glanced at her watch and noticed that she was an hour late. She was usually home by six p.m., but it was a quarter to six and she still had miles to walk.

She looked to the heavens and said a small prayer, and asked God to protect her and her children from all harm and to bless her husband. She knew why Nate was the way that he was. They owned their farm outright but, in Arkansas you were only as valuable as the color of your skin. Nate had the skin tone of a white man, but his kinky hair removed any doubt as to what his ethnicity was. He was the son of a fair skinned black mother that had been the mistress of her white boss. He was a bastard child, and he had hatred for all white people and he didn't trust any women. To him, women were tools meant to carry children, cook, and clean. No more, no less.

Every harvest Nate had to go to town to sell their crops, and no matter how beautiful the harvest, he was never given fair value. He was shortchanged for the eggs his hens produced and the milk that came from his cows. The unfairness ate at him and made him bitter, because as much as he wanted to, he couldn't say a word to the hillbilly white men in town for fear that they would burn his farm to the ground.

Nathaniel Gage was looked upon in town as a "good nigger". He dropped his head when talking to the white man and never made eye contact because to them, that was a sign of aggression. He took the abusive name calling and constant taunts with a mixture of disdain and fear.

He wondered which one of the old honkies in town was his father. He knew that they were aware of his origins and it angered him. He would do as most cowards did when faced with men that he either couldn't handle or wouldn't handle; he would merely go home and take it out on his wife and children.

Gertrude made it to her property line just as the sun was setting. She could see her husband sitting on the front porch in the wooden rocking chair that he had crafted by hand. He was looking out over the field with a menacing grimace on his face. Gertrude knew it was well after six and Nate was angry, but it wasn't her fault.

Her sons were performing their usual duties. They would milk the cows, collect eggs from the henhouse, and clean the barn before they were allowed inside the house to eat dinner.

Before Gertrude could make it to the front porch, Nathaniel abruptly stopped rocking, got up from his chair and walked inside. As soon as Gertrude stepped into the small, two-bedroom farmhouse, he slapped her to her knees. "Stand up and face me, cheating whore!" he spat.

Gertrude's head was spinning, and she couldn't focus her eyes. She looked up at her husband and could only see a blur of a man. She was only able to steal a quick glance before he struck her again but, this time with a closed fist, and everything went black.

She didn't know how long she had been out by the time he'd poured water in her face to wake her up. "Nathaniel, baby, listen! It started to rain so I stopped in the old Tucker family warehouse to wait the rain out! Please, baby I would never cheat on you!" Gertrude pleaded, but the anger had overtaken Nate as he pounded her.

Finally her body had gone limp. Nathaniel tried to revive her so that he could beat her more, but she wouldn't move. Her lifeless body was twisted into a heap of soulless flesh.

The heartless bastard hadn't even given her body time to cool; he simply dropped her body and walked to the tool shed, grabbed a shovel and started digging a grave behind their house, as if digging a grave for a dead pet. By lantern light he dug until the sweat covered his brow in huge beads of salty moisture.

Nathaniel was filled with both exhaustion and exhilaration. He had been chided and teased throughout his entire life, and he would be damned if he let his own wife laugh with the white man and then come home and lay in his bed.

Charles happily burst into the house. He was sure that he would see his mother's beautiful face greeting him as she did every night. He was anticipating her soft sweet voice, but when he entered he stopped in his tracks. Lying crumpled on the floor was his mother's lifeless body. Her eyes were open, staring into the abyss with no sign of life in them. Charles dropped to his knees next to his mother, hoping that she wasn't dead. He called to her softly and touched her face. Her skin had begun to cool. He knew in his young heart that she was gone. He knew that she was dead, and he knew who was responsible.

As he ran from the house full stride to get to his brothers, he took the rickety steps two at a time and fell face first at the bottom of the stairs. He sprang to his feet and continued his stride, screaming for his oldest brother at the top of his lungs. "Julius! Julius!" he screamed.

He found his brothers all huddled in the barn like rebellious slaves hatching a plan for escape.

Julius looked at his little brother's face and instantly panicked. Charles was a very cool little brother, and he never got excited about too much, so for him to be this upset there had to be something wrong. "What's wrong, little one?" he asked.

"It's Mama! She's lyin' on the flo' and she's not movin', Ju!" Charles exclaimed.

All four brothers started to move towards the house in trepidation. Julius reached the house first, and there on the floor just as Charles had said lay his mother, her face cradled by a nest of long, jet black hair. Blood was leaking from her head and seeped down between the wooden slats of the floor. Julius knew instantly that his father was responsible.

At thirteen, Julius was almost as tall as his father, if not taller. His young anger was apparent, and as his hatred started to build, his grief gave way to an overwhelming rage. He knew in his heart that his beautiful mother was dead. He stood over her body and silently wept. He didn't want his younger brothers to see him fall apart. He had always been the "father" to his siblings, because their father had no interest in holding that title.

Julius went to the corner by the couch and grabbed his father's .223 Winchester rifle and headed for the door. He knew exactly how to use the rifle, because in happier times his father had loved to take his sons hunting.

On Julius' heels were his three brothers. Charles had grabbed a box of ammunition from a nearby table, and Otha Lee and Eugene had armed themselves with knives from the kitchen drawer. None of the young boys knew what to expect from the encounter with their father, but one thing was certain; Nathaniel Gage would pay for what he had done to their mother.

As they rounded the corner of the house, near the shed they saw their father hard at work digging their mother's grave. Julius had always been very respectful of his father because that is the way that he was taught. But he loved his mother, and his father had taken that away.

Julius pointed the rifle at his father "What the fuck did you do to Mama!" he screamed.

Nathaniel looked at the young man with a dazed craziness in his eyes. "This here is grown folk's business, boy. You would do well to gon' in the house and tend to your brothers," his father stated calmly.

"Naw, old man, you got some answering to do. Me and these boys see everyday how you treated Mama. Now she's dead, so you need to tell us something, or you can sort it out with the Lord when you get to the Pearly Gates!" Julius spat.

The Gage patriarch threw his head back and laughed wildly and hysterically. "Boy, I been dead inside a long time. Between you boys and your triflin' ass mammy, I ain't lived in years. Do what you got to do, youngster," he said, hoping to call his oldest son's bluff. But inside he was terrified. There was something about the look in his son's eyes that told him that the boy was as serious as cancer.

Julius walked closer to his father and pointed the rifle in his face, nudging him slightly with the barrel of the gun in the forehead. "Get in that grave, old man!" he barked, poking at his father's head harder with the barrel.

Nathaniel pleaded with his son. "Julius, don't do this, son, please!" The desperation in his voice was evident. Nathaniel was a coward. He was the type of man that loved to pick on women and children, but he would never confront a man.

Julius was nobody's child. He looked at his father and started to cry. He didn't really know why he was crying. Maybe it was anger, maybe sadness, maybe from confusion, but whatever the case, he knew what had to be done. "Don't beg, you red bastard!" Julius pulled the trigger once, and his father's head exploded into a mass of blood and brains. It resembled the watermelons that he had used for target practice on so many occasions.

His father stumbled back and fell into the grave that he had so tirelessly and effortlessly dug for their mother.

Charles shrieked in fear but, quickly regained his composure.

Julius turned to his younger brothers, searching their faces for some sense of approval. They were so young and innocent, and now just as he's always done, he would take care of his little brothers the best way he knew how... by hook or crook.

Chapter 1

All that Jazz

Life for Julius Jr. was simple; clean your room and his Mama was happy; obey and be in church on time, and his Daddy was happy; stay out of the way, and his three sisters and two brothers were happy. But lately, life didn't seem so simple. His mother and father had been fighting a lot lately. He couldn't exactly put his finger on it because adult talk wasn't understandable all the time. But from what he heard and understood, with Daddy being a preacher, no wife of his was going to be a lounge singer. And from what Mama said, that's where he met her at before he became a holy roller.

Life in Benton Harbor seemed to be taking a turn, and not for the better. This night seemed especially tense. Julius' siblings' father had come to pick them up, and their father and Julius Sr. had gotten into a shouting match. His mother, Najé had not "checked" her ex like Julius Sr. thought she should, so arguments erupted. There were small arguments at first, and then bigger ones until finally, rumbling.

9

Julius Jr. ran and hid at first, but then he got angry. He ran through the house and up the stairs as fast as his little eight year old legs could carry him. When he got to the top of the stairs, what he saw made his heart cringe. His father was standing over his mother's body. Her arms were raised in defense and his father was holding a butcher knife. *What should I do?* he thought. In his little small, weak, eight year old voice he begged, "Daddy, please don't!"

Najé seized this as an opportunity, "Yeah, Daddy! Please don't! What are you going to do? Kill me in front of our son?" she said in a voice seething with sarcasm and contempt.

Julius Sr. looked at his son, then at his wife and back at his son again. "Junior, get your shit. We're leaving," he said.

And that was that.

There were no objections from Najé. *If he wants to take his son, so be it,* she thought. Hell, it was hard enough raising five, let alone six hungry bad ass kids. She had dreams, and those dreams didn't include six kids at thirty years old. No sir, there was more to life than living for men and kids, and she was going to prove it.

Julius Sr. was still angry, and in his mind it was a good thing that his son had walked in, because he was going to cut her from her ass to her appetite.

Julius Sr. had a lot of thinking to do. His leaving Najé would make him a single father and he worried about whether he could do it successfully. He was a long way from his days as a younger man. He had been a hustler, a thief, an enforcer, and a mercenary for hire so to speak, and his brutality was legendary. He had once killed a man with his bare hands and hadn't left a trace of evidence. He had been paid handsomely for his ruthlessness, and he was known to be impeccably accurate with his killing skills. But things were different now. He wasn't just living for himself; he now held two lives in his hands.

Things had changed since Najé had told Julius that she was pregnant. He had accepted her children as his own, as well as embracing the thought of having a new baby. He was more excited about the thought of being a father, he reasoned, than Najé seemed to be, but it was of no consequence to him. If she didn't want the baby, then he would gladly raise it on his own. He didn't care whether the child was a boy or a girl; his new seed would know the full love of a father.

Julius had secrets that he couldn't share with anyone. They were dark secrets that he would most likely carry to his grave, but nevertheless they were his secrets.

Now, after years of being away from Dallas he was going back. In Texas he had made many friends, but for every friend that he'd made, there were just as many enemies. He wasn't too concerned about the foes he had accumulated over the years because they knew his reputation, and his reputation was solid.

There were certain things that he needed his son to know, but his mind was young and delicate and too fragile to process the information that his father had to share with him

Caught up in his own thoughts, Julius didn't notice the steady stream of tears running down his son's face or the blank sullen look in his eyes.

Jr. was going to miss his mother, his siblings, and most of all he was going to miss their big house on Pavone Boulevard. He had heard his father talking to his uncle about Texas before. *Texas? Wasn't that cows and horses and ranches?* Well, no matter where they were going, Jr. had made up his mind to hate it. He wasn't riding any horses or making any friends. He hated Texas with a passion and he hadn't even touched the soil yet. But what he did know was that his family was splitting up, so in his young mind he thought, *"Fuck Texas!"*

Chapter 2

New Beginnings

South Dallas Texas didn't look anything like Benton Harbor, and Julius damn sure didn't see any ranches or horses. What he saw was ghetto on top of ghetto. He and his father pulled up in front of a small, two-story wood framed house on Pine Street, and his father blew the horn and his Uncle Charlie Boy came outside.

Charlie Boy was younger than his father was, but it was amazing how much the two looked alike. Julius Sr. was 5'11", about 225lbs., dark skinned, with strong features and graying hair. Charlie Boy was the exact same, but his hair was not graying and he weighed about 185lbs. on a boxer's frame.

"Ju, what's up, bruh?" Charlie asked.

"Not a thang, Charlie Boy. Just ready for a fresh start, you know? I'm ready to put this bullshit behind me and get on with me and my son's life," Julius exclaimed.

"Yeah, I hear that shit, but listen. I got some topnotch playas I want you to meet... some connected niggas."

"Charlie, you know I straightened my life out and gave it to the Lord. I'm not trying to get caught up in my old earthly ways," Julius said.

"Yeah, nigga, I hear you talking, but you still got to feed that youngster. And the last I heard, Jesus wasn't givin' no credit!"

They both laughed like it was an old inside joke, but Julius Jr. didn't find it funny. He was tired, and it seemed like they had rode forever. During the long ride, he would go to sleep and wake up and see lights, go to sleep, wake up to take a piss, go to sleep, wake up to see trees, and finally they had pulled into their destination in his father's new Ford LTD.

The "dream car" was cream yellow with a peanut butter rag top, crystal-clear windows, and suede peanut butter interior. Julius Sr. was proud to drive it, and Lil' Julius was proud to ride in it. It rode like a dream, so his father called it "The Dream Car".

Now that they were finally at their destination, all Lil' Julius wanted to do was go to sleep and start fresh tomorrow.

Uncle Charlie Boy didn't have kids, but he did have a wife, Aunt Pearl, who was the spitting image of Pam Grier. She was Lil' Julius' favorite aunt because she actually reminded him of his mother. Plus, she never seemed to run out of money and she loved to spend it on her "Ju-Ju Bean" as she called him.

When Aunt Pearl saw Lil' Julius' face, she lit up like a Christmas tree. She ran out to the car, grabbed him and kissed him and hugged him like she hadn't seen him forever. The truth is, she had just seen him last summer when he spent summer vacation with her and Charlie Boy.

Lil' Julius was still trying to figure out why grownups would spend money on bags of grass. His uncle and aunt seemed to make a lot of money selling grass in bags. They called it "reefer", but it looked like grass to him. *Well, grass was evidently a good business,* he thought, because Uncle Charlie Boy drove a new Cadillac.

Aunt Pearl had to be a special lady because she knew everyone. "Hey, Pearl, baby!" "Hey, Pearly!" "Hey, sweetie!" people would say. No matter where she went, people spoke to Aunt Pearl, and even when she was angry she managed a smile and a polite, "Hey, sugar!" right back in their direction.

He would catch his uncle and aunt fighting sometimes, but it was never too serious, like his mother and father's fights. They used to argue about small things, like why Aunt Pearl let Ju-Ju stay up so late, and why Uncle Charlie used to talk to Ju-Ju about guns. It was like the only time they argued at all was when he was around, because all of the arguments seemed to stem from him.

But now he could see Aunt Pearl every day, and it was still summer so school wouldn't start for a while.

He noticed that his aunt and uncle didn't work regular jobs. They sold weed, and late at night people would come by to buy beer and whiskey. But they never got up in the mornings and went to work like "normal" people did.

Pearl always made sure Julius Jr.'s bath water was just right. It always smelled like cherry bubbles. As he was sitting in the tub playing with bubbles he could hear people talking; not his father and uncle, but other voices:

"Listen, Julius. You can work for us running the joint, and we'll pay you $500 a week plus $5 off of every bottle you sell," Rabbit said.

"Rabbit, that sounds out of sight. Five hundred a week is some nice bread, but I have to think about my boy, you dig?"

"Yeah, Ju, I dig it, but let's be honest. You ain't getting no younger and jobs ain't going to jump out of the trees for you, nigga," Rabbit said.

Big Julius thought for a minute, and then said "Okay, bruh, but no illegal stuff. I'm through with that lifestyle."

Rabbit and his partner, Booty Green looked at one another with a sly grin, and with a nod all the men shook hands.

Pearl walked into the bathroom to check on Julius, and once she was satisfied that he was okay she closed the door. She turned to Charlie Boy and Julius and whispered, "I don't trust them niggas, man. Rabbit makes me uneasy with that gold ass smile and blue eyes. And Booty Green would just as soon kill you than shake your hand."

Julius put his arm around her shoulder and said in a voice that was neither fearful nor apprehensive, "Don't worry, sis-in-law. I can handle it. Besides, Rabbit and Booty Green know me, and they won't disrespect my wishes."

"Okay, if you say you got it, I'ma trust you. But be careful, Julius," Pearl warned.

Once Lil' Julius was out of the bathtub, Pearl settled him into bed. A bed had never felt so good to the tired boy. He was almost instantly asleep, but before he could fully go to sleep he had to hear his Aunty Pearl sing. She always sang the same song. It reminded him of his sister, Kitty, and it reminded him of safety.

Before Pearl could finish the whole song, Ju-Ju was fast asleep. Pearl looked down at her nephew, only eight years old, and noticed that even at such an early age he was the spitting image of Julius, Charlie Boy and their brothers. She chuckled at the thought of the many memories that she had of her Ju-Ju Bean, and then just as quickly got depressed at the realization that she couldn't have any children of her own. *That's okay,* she thought. *As long as I have Ju-Ju, he's as good as my own.* She tucked in the covers as she often did and kissed his forehead, but before she closed the door she stole one last glance at him and noticed that the moonlight shining through the window cast an almost angelic glow on her "chocolate angel".

17

Chapter 3

Business as Usual

Once downstairs, Pearl set about her nightly routine: start Charlie Boy a pot of coffee, set out the nickel, dime, and twenty bags of reefer, put ice on the beer and whiskey, and make Charlie Boy's dinner. Tonight she would make a special dinner though, because tonight was kind of an anniversary. Tonight five years ago, Charlie Boy came into the strip club, saw her and talked to her like no man had ever talked to her before. He had told her he wasn't like the rest of the niggas that came in there. He made her feel like a woman, not a piece of meat, and he told her the world could be hers if she trusted in him. By the time Charlie Boy left she felt like a million dollars. He had come back to see her a few days later and said he wanted to take her out on a "real date," instead of just seeing her titties and ass.

At first she was skeptical because she had just gotten away from her pimp, Yellow Shoes, and Charles Gage looked like a stone cold player. Charlie was a player, but he was a different type of player who called himself a "finesse player", not a "broad player" like all the other players that Pearl knew. She had said yes to the date, and was glad that she did because he was a complete gentleman.

He took her to what he believed to be a nice restaurant—not quite what she thought a nice restaurant was—but still, Wyatt's Cafeteria had good food and good service. It wasn't like the cheap rundown burger joints like Good Luck Burgers that she was used to. She hated those places because they were always so greasy and they made her feel sick to her stomach.

It seemed like until she met Charlie she had never known a real man, but he was just that; a man. He was not afraid to talk, not afraid to speak his mind, but most importantly he had promised not to hit her. He said that from that day forward his mission was to make her happy, and he held true to his word.

A hard knock at the door had awakened Pearl from her daydream, and she needed to start dinner soon anyway. "Who is it?" she barked.

"It's Chele, girl! Open the damn door!"

"Damn, honey! You knocking like the police and shit! Hell!"

"I heard that your fine ass brother-in-law was back in town," Chele said.

"Yeah, he's back." Pearl gave Chele a look of mixed admiration and disgust.

Chele was a beautiful woman, but she tried too hard. She was light skinned and had long silky hair. She stood about 5'3", 120lbs., and was stacked like a brick shit house.

Pearl knew that Julius would never have her because he saw her for what she really was; just a pretty face, nothing more and nothing less. She wasn't his type. In his eyes, a woman that didn't have children didn't have any sense of responsibility, and most certainly couldn't be trusted to care for Lil' Julius.

But it wasn't Pearl's place to kill the young girl's dreams of having a man like Julius. Chele was three years older than Pearl was, and at twenty seven years old she still acted like an adolescent at times. It was amazing to Pearl how a woman could have lived twenty seven years, and her biggest aspiration was to land a man that didn't want her.

Pearl had started "hoing" at fifteen because she wanted nice clothes to wear to school and food to eat. It started with a few select boys at school first, but once the older men found out, they wanted it and were willing to pay more. Then she met Yellow Shoes, and her life began to tumble downhill.

When Yellow went to prison, she was just about to graduate from high school, and he had wasted all of the money she'd ever hustled. Pearl went straight into stripping from high school, and a year later she'd met Charlie Boy and she couldn't be happier. She was happy for a change, and she vowed to do anything in her power to keep Charlie Boy happy with her. He had saved her when nobody else gave a damn. He had been her father, her mother, her best friend, and the gentlest lover she'd ever known.

Charlie Boy was the real deal, and she often felt ashamed for him because everyone knew that he was married to a former whore. But her husband would always tell her, "Pearly, baby, everybody deserves a second chance. Why should you be any different? Besides, you're the best thing that ever happened to me, and you're more real than half these so-called square bitches out here that are only out for themselves."

She had heard him check a couple of his so-called friends when they boldly informed him that he couldn't turn a hoe into a housewife. She had to chuckle at Charlie Boy's response because it was harsh but intelligently put:

"Nigga, I would rather have an ex hoe that got it out of her system than to be blind like you dumb ass niggas and be married to some tired, broke, unhappy bitches that give up the pussy out of both panty legs as soon as you fuck-boys leave the house!" And he added for weight, "As a matter of fact, since you disrespectful ass niggas don't have respect for my wife, you can leave!"

She blushed at the thought of it, because no man had ever stood up for her before unless it had to do with money. But Charles Boyd Gage had done it because he loved him some Pearl, and she intended to make sure that he never had to regret his decision.

Pearl told Chele that Julius and Charlie Boy were out on business and that they wouldn't be back for a while, but she was more than welcome to stay and wait.

"Naw, girl. I'll just see him later or something. Just gimme a nick sack and a pint of E & J. Oh, and tell Julius' fine ass I said call me."

Pearl just smiled and said, "Uh-huh, okay, honey."

Chapter 4

Daddy's Baby

Chele had come from very humble beginnings. She was the daughter of a Baptist minister and a housewife. Her father was strict on her to the point that it was almost unbearable. Chele's mother followed her father around like a puppy on a leash, and Chele had made up her mind that she would never be so blindly in love like that with any man.

For years she had been a model child. She got good grades in school, she was in the church choir, and she helped out around the house with chores. Her mother had high hopes for their only daughter, but with age came change. As Chele hit her teenaged years, her body had started to change and everyone around her noticed. She got attention from all directions, and grown men noticed her body more than anyone else.

It wasn't long before rumors had started to circulate about Chele having sex with older men, but they were just that; rumors. She was a proud virgin. After all, her father had told her that good girls waited until they were married to have sex, so she wasn't in any hurry because she was saving herself for her future husband.

Because of the rumors, she and her father had been into it heavy. He didn't believe a word she said and she was getting tired of it. She didn't have a reason to lie to him, but he was relentless with the pressure. She had always been his "little girl", and now he was treating her as if he didn't even know her.

It was beginning to be unbearable, and it seemed as though everyone she knew hated her. The girls in her school hated her because she was beautiful, the guys never let up with the constant taunts and touching, but the older men were the worst with their leers, whistles and muffled flirts. She only wanted to go to school and do as she was told.

She had to admit that the attention was flattering. She giggled inside to think that all of these men wanted her for a girlfriend. She was a naïve young girl and she knew it.

Chele was in her room ironing her dress for church on a particularly brisk Saturday night, when she heard her mother and father in the next room arguing. Their house was small, only a few sparse rooms with shoddy furniture, and the walls were paper thin. She could tell from the tone in her father's voice that he had been drinking. She could only shake her head. He would go to church on Sundays, preaching about the body being a temple for Christ but, during the week he was usually drunk.

Chele could hear bits and pieces of the argument;
"...She's a good girl," said her mother.
"She's gonna hafta learn..." her father shot back.

They had to be talking about her, but why? She hadn't done anything wrong. She had done all of her chores and she never ever talked to any of the men or boys that flirted with her.

After ironing her clothes that night, she had taken a shower and lay in bed wondering what the other teenagers in her town were doing. She also wondered what the big deal was about when it came to sex.

Her parents had gotten quiet and all of the lights in the small house were out.

Chele closed her eyes and tried to picture what it must feel like to have sex. As her imagination took over, her nipples on her firm breasts started to stiffen. She was only fifteen but, her body had developed into that of a grown woman. She let her small soft hands glide over her firm body, finding their way to her crotch. She could feel the moisture through her cotton panties. Her heart was racing, but there was no turning back. She put her hand inside of her panties and felt the moist, wet, slippery feeling of her womanhood. She allowed her finger to slip inside and she gasped from pleasure. She tried two fingers but they wouldn't fit, so she settled for the one finger and experienced even more pleasure. Fast then slow; deep then shallow, she was lost in a world of self-lust.

The experience was mind-blowing. She couldn't believe how good it felt. It was as though her body was on fire and her insides were on a rollercoaster ride of ecstasy. As she neared her climatic end she kicked the blanket off and bucked wildly in anticipation of what was to come.

Her self-satisfying sexual fantasy was interrupted by her father bursting through her door. He stood in the doorway of his daughter's small bedroom, naked, with his manhood fully erect.

Chele reached for the blanket to cover her nakedness, but her father moved quickly and snatched it away. She screamed from a mixture of surprise and nervousness.

With one clumsy hand her father ripped her panties from her body.

"Daddy, stop! Please! Daddy, don't do this, please!" she pleaded.

Her father was in a drunken daze, not hearing his daughter's pleas. He mounted her and thrust himself violently inside of her. She couldn't think. She tried to push him off of her but, he was too heavy.

"You running around here like you grown, so I'm gon' treat you like you grown, girl!" her father spat lustily in her ear.

Chele couldn't believe her own father was raping her. She called out to her mother. "Mama, please! Help me! Get Daddy off me!" Her mother didn't answer, but Chele knew she had to be awake. She woke up every time her father shifted in bed, let alone if he got out of the bed.

Chele could no longer fight. She sadly lay back and let her father have his way with her. She felt so violated, and he was thrusting and gyrating wildly. The pain was intense and she just wished that it was over.

Finally after what seemed like hours, her father had exited her room, leaving her in a puddle of his semen and her blood.

She never spoke of it, and both her mother and father acted as if the incident never happened. But it had happened, and a few months later, Chele's stomach bore the evidence of that night. Neither her mother nor her father ever mentioned her pregnancy. Chele was devastated. She had always held her father in the highest regard, and for him to violate her that way soiled her opinion of him. Her mother's image was tarnished also. Was her mother so afraid of her dad that she would allow this to happen?

She had just started to show when her mother and father came to her with a hundred dollars and a bus ticket to Dallas, Texas. There were no explanations, no apologies... nothing. Her parents were more concerned with saving their name in the church than they were with her safety and well-being. Her mother had told her in not so subtle terms that her pregnancy was an embarrassment to the family.

Chele had sucked her teeth and rolled her eyes and said, "If your husband hadn't raped me I wouldn't be pregnant, Mama!"

Her mother slapped her face and turned and walked away.

As Chele packed her clothes to leave, her mother had come into her room and sat on her bed. "I'm sorry, Michele. I haven't always been a good mother, but I do love you. What your father did to you is unforgivable, but he is my husband and your father!"

"I don't have a father, Mama! My father died the night he took my childhood!" Chele wept.

"At any rate," Chele's mother began. "I want you to take care of yourself, and if you ever need me, I am here." She stood to leave and gave one last glance at her daughter. "I love you, baby."

Chele didn't know whether she was hurt or relieved, or both. What she did know was that she was fifteen years old and pregnant, had a tenth grade education and didn't know the first thing about raising a child.

She exited the Trailways bus not knowing in the least what to expect from the city life in Dallas, Texas. It was early morning before sunrise, and the city lights bounced dreamily off of the dew-covered asphalt of the downtown streets. The crisp autumn air mixed with the aroma of home cooking took control of her senses. She remembered that she hadn't eaten since she left home the day before. She walked into a diner and looked around. There were mostly white folks inside, which in itself made her nervous. If Dallas was anything like her hometown, then black people and white people did not mix.

"Are you lost, girl?" an old white man asked.

"Yes sir, actually I am. Can you tell me where the black folks congregate in this city, please?"

There was an eruption of laughter and chuckles throughout the diner. The old man came from behind the counter with his grease stained apron and holding a spatula in one hand and a cigarette in the other. "Congregate, huh? That's a mighty fancy word for a nigger, even if you are a pretty one!" The man laughed.

Chele felt her blood boil, but she held her composure. "I just need to know how to get to my own kind, sir," she said. Her irritation was evident, and everyone inside the small establishment knew it.

"Get your little black ass on that 44 Oakland bus, and you'll be in South Dallas. And little lady, never in your life come back to my diner!" the man said with a southern drawl straight out of "Gone with the Wind".

Chele managed to utter an almost inaudible "Thank you" as she exited the diner.

She had no idea where she was going when she got on the city bus. She thought that she would just ride until she saw some black people.

She looked out of the bus window and noticed a section on the corner of Pine Street and Colonial Boulevard that looked busy. On the crowded streets, men and women were rushing to their jobs, so Chele decided that this would be about as good of a place as any to start her new life.

She stepped out into the early morning light of day and took a deep breath and looked around as if to take in her surroundings. She spotted Clara's Kitchen. She hadn't gotten the chance to eat at the diner downtown, because the way the owner was talking, they probably didn't serve blacks anyway. She walked into Clara's and sat in a corner booth at the back of the restaurant.

"Hey, sugar. Welcome to Clara's. Can I get you sum'n?" an older gray haired woman asked.

"Um, can I have some toast and a cup of coffee, please?"

The waitress looked at the young woman. "I don't know, baby. Can you?" Miss Clara teased.

"I mean, *may* I have a cup of coffee and toast, please?" Chele said, obviously embarrassed by her slip in manners.

"Yes, you may, but do you think you need to be drinking coffee in your condition?" Concern showed on the lady's old but pretty face.

Chele started to cry. She hadn't given much thought to the fact that she was pregnant, and the thought of it was too much weight for her to carry. She sat in the corner booth sobbing until the table was almost covered in tears.

Clara sat next to the young girl and placed her arms around her to comfort her. "What's wrong, baby?" she asked.

Chele started rambling and talking in circles, and to Clara, she was not making much sense. Maybe if she took her to the back office the child would be more willing to open up and talk to her. Clara motioned for Chele to follow her. On the way to the office, she grabbed the girl a cup of coffee, a few slices of toast and a couple of strips of bacon.

Once inside her office, Clara closed the door and invited the girl to have a seat.

Chele was somewhat composed and able to talk. She told the woman how she always tried to live up to her father's expectations. She told her how she seemed to never be able to depend on her mother. And finally, she had told her how her Baptist preacher father had raped her, gotten her pregnant, and then sent her away. By the time she was finished recounting the tale they were both in tears.

Miss Clara looked into the beautiful young girl's eyes and told her that if she would trust her, then she would help her as much as she could.

"Thank you, Miss Clara. I won't let you down, I promise," Chele said.

Clara hugged her and said, "You lie on that couch over there and get you some rest. After my breakfast rush we'll talk about what you wanna do about that child you're carrying."

Chele allowed herself to doze off and drift into a peaceful sleep. Even though she was convinced that her father was an evil man, he had been right about one thing; you never knew when God would send one of his angels to rescue you at your lowest point.

After the morning breakfast rush, Clara returned to the office to find the young girl fast asleep. She sat at her desk and watched her. She was a really pretty girl, and Clara felt sorry for her. She knew exactly what she had to do to help her new friend. She nudged Chele gently. "Wake up, baby. We got a lot to do today."

Chele opened her eyes to see Clara standing across the room, removing her apron and smoothing the wrinkles in her dress. She wondered silently to herself why the woman was so eager to help her. It entered her mind that maybe she was some kind of pervert that liked young girls, but she just as quickly dismissed the notion. If the woman was willing to help her, then she wouldn't look a gift horse in the mouth.

Clara took Chele to her house. She couldn't believe her eyes because the home was beautiful. It wasn't huge, but it wasn't small either. It was surrounded by a wooden fence. The grass was as green as sapphires, and there were flowers of every color in the front yard. She could tell that the elderly woman took great pride in her garden.

The inside of Clara's house smelled like fresh fruit and expensive perfume. It reminded Chele of her grandmother's house.

"Make yourself at home, baby," Clara offered.

Chele sat on the plush couch. It was white and wrapped in plastic, but comfortable nevertheless.

From the kitchen Clara yelled, "So, what are we gonna do about this youngin' you're carrying, child?"

"Well, I can't very well carry my own daddy's baby, Miss Clara," Chele said, trying hard to mask her sarcasm.

"I may have a solution, dear heart."

"I sure hope so, Miss Clara. I don't know what to do." Chele had begun to cry again. She could hear Clara talking on the phone in the kitchen, but she couldn't make out the conversation.

Clara came into the front room where Chele was seated and took a seat next to her. "I have friends in very high places, lovey. I also have an equal amount of friends in very low places. And because you're under aged we are going to utilize some of those friends," Clara stated.

Chele had no idea what the woman was talking about, but she would listen to her. After all, she had nothing else to lose.

Clara explained to her that her friends would perform a procedure called an "abortion", and no one ever needed to know.

Later that night under a veil of darkness, Clara took Chele to a section of town that looked industrial and abandoned. They parked the car on a dark deserted street and walked down a dreary desolate alleyway.

Clara gave two stiff knocks on a heavy steel door. Waiting for a response seemed to take a lifetime and Clara seized it as an opportunity to talk to Chele. "Don't be nervous, child. Just do as they say and it will be quick and easy."

A small nimble Chinese man with a white doctor's coat answered the door and ushered the two women inside. "You pay half now, half when finish," he said in broken English.

Clara handed the man a wad of cash and watched as he walked away. Moments later they were shown into a room that was empty except for a stainless steel gurney and a stainless steel table filled with surgical instruments.

Chele was given a hospital gown and instructed to undress, lie on the table and relax. She did as she was told. As she lay there, she could feel the coldness of the steel gurney and she could smell the faint odor of old blood.

The Chinese doctor entered the room and put an oxygen mask over Chele's face and asked her to count backwards from ten. She began to count: "Ten, nine, eight, seven, six..."

Clara stood next to her, holding her hand.

"Five, four, three..." Chele could see bloody towels in the corner of the cold dark room: "Two, one..." And then darkness. *Hopefully this would all be over soon,* she thought as she drifted into nothingness.

Chapter 5

Young Girl Lost

Pearl had often tried to explain her love for Chele to her husband, but she wasn't sure if Charlie really understood. Pearl and Chele had many things in common, and their past circumstances were relatively the same.

The first time Pearl met Chele both girls were involved with Yellow Shoes, except that Chele was in with him a lot deeper than Pearl happened to be.

When Yellow Shoes went away to prison Pearl saw it as a blessing, but Chele had stayed by his side, riding his time out with him as though she was trying to be a wife to the man that had turned her out and made her a whore. To Pearl Chele's loyalty to the pimp was misplaced and unnatural.

There was nothing glamorous about the lives that they lived, and on more than one occasion they had both sat and talked and cried about the what if's of getting out of the game. Sadly enough when the opportunity had presented itself, Chele was less than willing to sever her ties with the street pimp. It was as if she wasn't satisfied until she'd lost everything and everyone that was in her corner. But Pearl had proven herself to be a loyal friend.

Mrs. Clara had long since washed her hands of the young girl after trying to shield her from the harsh realities of street life in South Dallas. Yellow Shoes had come into Clara's Kitchen early one morning after hearing about the "bad yella bone" that was working in the diner.

Chele was young, sexy and very naïve, and to have a grown man as handsome as Yellow Shoes to actually show her attention was, in her mind, somehow a compliment. She lacked self-worth, and her self-esteem was so low that one would swear that she was 5'1" and 600-lbs. Nevertheless she was smitten by Yellow Shoes, and she was captivated by his every word.

Mrs. Clara had warned her about who Yellow Shoes was, what he did for a living and of his ruthless and less than stellar reputation, but to no avail. Chele was so taken by him that she had started to compromise her position at Clara's Kitchen by showing up late, if she showed up at all. She would fight with anyone that had a bad word to say about Yellow Shoes, and things had finally come to a head with Chele and Mrs. Clara when money had started to come up missing from the diner's safe.

Clara had always trusted Chele. She treated her as if she were her own flesh and blood; the daughter that she never had, so to speak. It was unthinkable to Clara that her "daughter" would steal from her for the love of a man that made his money from the sweat and bodies of so many innocent young girls. Love was truly blind, but as Mrs. Clara reasoned love was nobody's fool.

Before she confronted Chele, she wanted to be sure that in her old age she wasn't miscounting her money. She wanted to be certain that what she felt and what she knew were one and the same. Even when some of the other women that worked at the diner had come to her and encouraged her to keep an eye on the young waitress and her sticky fingers, she had abruptly declined. The way Clara saw it, why would Chele steal from her when she had done everything in her power to help the young girl? She was hurt by her suspicions because she wanted and needed to believe in Chele.

Not having children of her own had always left a void in her heart, so when Chele came along and needed her she had jumped in, full steam ahead. Clara had invited the girl into her home and into her life, essentially making her heir apparent to all that she had to offer.

After years of molding her young protégé, Clara was sure that Chele was ready to take over Clara's Kitchen. But only one roadblock prevented her from turning over complete control of the diner to Chele, and his name was Yellow Shoes.

Instead of Clara accusing Chele of theft, she tried her hardest to give her the benefit of the doubt. She wanted to know for certain before the confrontation. Clara felt it in her gut though, and her gut was seldom wrong.

The plan was simple: She would tell Chele that she was leaving for the night like she always did, but instead of actually leaving she would double back, enter through the back door and wait in her office closet. She would leave the closet door cracked just enough to have a clear view of the safe and her desk. Chele would come in sit at the desk and tally the entire day's profits. If she was on the up and up,

35

she would put the money inside of the bank pouch and put it inside the safe, and then meet Mrs. Clara at home as she often did before heading out for a night on the town with Yellow Shoes.

Clara had gone over the plan in her head what seemed like a million times. Her suspicions had to be masked totally in order to keep Chele in her comfort zone, and just as she had hoped, Chele hadn't suspected a thing.

Clara took a perch in her closet and waited patiently. She had begun to doze off when she heard voices enter the office. Chele entered first, followed closely by Yellow Shoes. The events that followed left Clara confused and angry. Chele talked about her and the diner as if she was some common street whore that had never helped her or cared for her:

"...Fuck that old bitch, baby! She treats you like you're her flunky or something," Yellow Shoes said casually.

"I know, Shoes. She thinks I wanna work in this greasy ass diner my whole fucking life. I want the money from it, and that's all!" Chele spat.

"So you shouldn't have no problem giving me that money. Shit, all of this is gonna be yours one day, baby. Just look at it as a cash advance," Yellow Shoes mused.

"That's why I love you, Daddy! You're so smart!" the young girl said flirtatiously.

As Clara sat in the closet listening to the two of them, she couldn't believe her ears. How could Chele think that way?

Chele didn't even bother to count the money. She simply took a handful of Clara's hard earned money and gave it to the pimp.

From his inside jacket pocket Yellow Shoes produced a small plastic baggie with a white powdery substance inside. He cleared off Clara's desk and poured the powder out onto a plate that he had brought in from the diner. He scooped up a small amount with the long fingernail of his pinky finger and carefully placed it to his nostril. Then he repeated the process for his young lover. He had the young girl in the palm of his hands, and he knew it.

Clara sprang from the closet, outraged and unable to contain her anger any longer. "Chele, you are worthless! Can't you see that this two-bit hustler is playing you?" she screamed.

Chele was obviously surprised, but the drugs in her system caused her reaction to be slow and nonchalant. "See, baby? This is the shit I'm talking about. This old bitch don't know when to butt out!" Chele said to Yellow Shoes.

They both laughed, as if Clara had somehow done something wrong.

"I want you both out of here or I am calling the police! Chele, I want your things out of my house before I return!" Clara said, and as she turned to leave, she looked at the pair in dazed confusion, and with tears of anger and hurt streaming down her cheeks. She added one last statement. "And Chele, if there is anything missing from my house, I will send the law after you!"

Clara left the diner, heart heavy from the pain of her adopted daughter's betrayal, but feeling somewhat relieved of a burden that was not hers to carry in the first place.

And just like that, Chele was out of Clara's life.

Yellow Shoes sat back with a sly grin on his face. He knew that without Clara in the picture he was free to turn

Chele into a world class whore. He had already started to turn her out. Now playtime was definitely over.

Chapter 6

'Bout That Paper

Charlie Boy and Julius pulled up in front of the R.C. Lounge and parked.

Charlie Boy gave Julius a long hard look, and with measured thought he chose his words carefully. "Ju, man, listen. I know you can handle your business, but these niggas are gangsters, mane."

Julius gave his brother a devious smirk and bluntly stated, "Nigga, me too. Rabbit and Green know me from the old days, and they would rather slide down a razor blade into a pool of alcohol than to fuck with me. Damn! You making me cuss! Let's go, baby boy."

Charlie knew Julius was right. His brother was a killer—not the psycho kind, but the calculated kind. It gave Charlie Boy chills to think of some of the things his brother had done. Julius always confided in him because they had a special bond.

Charlie was the youngest and Julius was the oldest. There were four brothers and no sisters, and all of them were equally as dangerous.

When Charlie Boy was five years old his father had kill their mother. And then minutes later he watched Julius kill their father. He remembered, but then he didn't remember.

Ever since that day, Julius had been everything to them... a mother, father, friend, disciplinarian, counselor and teacher. It had been Julius who taught each brother how to kill and do it effectively and quietly.

For Charlie Boys first lesson, Julius had taken him on a job in Little Rock, Arkansas. A man owed an associate of Julius' upward of twenty-thousand dollars, and Julius went to collect because his associate had told him that if he collected it, he could keep it. He explained he was a "paper made nigga", and he didn't care about the money. It was the principle of it.

Julius had followed his mark to an after-hours joint and knew he'd be in there for a while. They were parked about forty yards from the victim's car. After he and Charlie Boy were certain that the coast was clear, Julius took a thick gauge wire, some putty and a knife and crawled under his victim's car. He emerged a few moments later, sweating as he jogged back to their car.

When the victim came out and started his car, it exploded.

Charlie Boy could still remember their car shaking from the blast, and the grin of satisfaction on his older brother's face. It gave him chills then, and it gave him chills now.

As they entered the R.C. Lounge all eyes were on the brothers.

Julius noticed that time seemed to stand still as they walked in. Charlie was dressed in royal blue silk with alligator shoes, and Julius was decked out in a cream colored leisure suit with a matching Dobbs hat and Stacy Adams. They nodded to a few people and were immediately ushered into the back office, where Rabbit and Green were waiting.

"Come in, fellas," Rabbit greeted. "Come in and have a seat. Can I get you something to drink?"

"Maybe later. So, what exactly does this job entail?" Julius asked nonchalantly.

"Well, the cover job is a barkeep. The only thing you have to do is manage the bar. I have a girl named Marie that bartends and waitresses, and she can assist you with anything you might need."

Julius looked at Rabbit and then at Green, and in a hushed but calculating tone asked, "Is that it?"

"Yeah, nigga. Why are you so damned paranoid, Ju?" Green asked.

Julius turned and walked away. Charlie followed close behind his brother, but he was still careful to keep his eyes open for the double cross. Charlie knew that Julius had a lot of enemies, but he also knew that just as many people that hated and feared him loved him also, because he was a good man.

He wondered why his brother had come back to South Dallas in the first place. South Dallas was one big ghetto as far as Charlie was concerned, and everything was sectioned off. There was the downtown section, and blacks didn't really go downtown unless they were going to pay bills or

41

going to the cheap department store, H.L. Green. Downtown was for the whites and the stores reflected it. Joske's, Sanger Harris and Neiman Marcus amongst others were expensive stores that the average black person couldn't afford.

Then you had East Dallas and Sunny South Dallas. These neighborhoods had just as many liquor stores as they did churches, and not nearly enough schools. South Dallas was divided into sections, and to be caught outside of your section was a dangerous situation.

Dixon Circle sat on the edge of South Dallas, Pleasant Grove and East Dallas. It was the most feared neighborhood on the south side. Then there was Bon Ton, the second most feared.

The other neighborhoods were much smaller but equally as dangerous, because it seemed as though everybody had something to prove. Grand Ave., Park Row, Pine and Colonial, and Oakland Ave. were merely streets where most of the gangsters and hoodlums hung out.

Charlie was a Pine and Colonial nigga through and through, and that pissed Julius off because he would always tell him, "Baby brother, don't be satisfied with neighborhood money, because Dallas is a big city with lots of money." But the south side was home. It was where everybody knew Charlie Boy, where he had met Pearl, and where he made his bread.

Julius had a thing or two to learn about neighborhood loyalty. Hell, Ju had always been a rolling stone. But not Charlie. Shit the south side had always been good to him. He was pulling in about $4,500 a week in profits, so he was good. But he knew his brother, and good was never enough. Julius had always taught him that good could be better, and better could be best, so he knew it was only a matter of time before Julius was out for the real money, and South Dallas was going to pay for it in a big way.

Julius was lost in thought, and so was Charlie Boy. They had no way of knowing that they were both thinking the exact same thing, about the exact same subject… getting that money in Sunny South Dallas.

Chapter 7

Gray Skies

The first day of school at Pearl C. Anderson Elementary School was different to say the least. Lil' Ju had stayed in the Pine and Colonial district, so he just knew he would be going to Phyllis Wheatley with the kids from the neighborhood, but his father had told him no, he was going to Pearl C. because they were moving to Dixon Circle, and that way he wouldn't have to transfer.

This morning he had awakened to the smell of bacon and eggs and his father's homemade biscuits. He got up, washed his face, brushed his teeth and couldn't wait to put on his new school clothes. He ate first, then went to iron and get dressed. Even though he was eight years old, his father treated him like a big boy and he liked that. He came out of his room and asked, "How do I look, Daddy?"

Big Ju looked at his son, with his jeans, new sneakers and "Dukes of Hazard" T-shirt and had to smile. *That boy's got the mind of a grown man,* he thought. "Looking good, Junior... looking good!"

They climbed into the "dream car" and drove the fifteen minutes to Pearl C. Anderson.

Before Ju-Ju got out of the car his father looked at him and smiled. "Here's a dollar, Junior, in case you want a snack or need anything, okay?"

"Okay, Daddy."

"Hey, what's the bread rule?" Julius Sr. yelled after him.

"Always pay yourself first, and never get broke!" his son yelled back. "Love you, Daddy! Bye!"

"See you later, mane. Never say good-bye!"

Ju-Ju turned gave his father a smile and ran inside the school.

He went to the principal's office and got his schedule. His teacher would be Mrs. Gray, and he hoped that she was nice. As he walked down the hall to room 207 he tried to take in as much as possible because his father had always told him know your surroundings.

He noticed the new school year decorations, and the teachers standing in their doorways welcoming the kids. Some of the kids were clean, some where dirty, some smiled, and some didn't.

He reached room 207, and Mrs. Gray looked young like aunt Pearl. Julius thought that she was very pretty. She looked like an angel, in a red dress with red framed glasses, and she had a distinctive gray streak in her hair.

"Hello, sweetie. Are you going to go in and have a seat, or are you going to stand there and look at me all day?"

"Sorry, ma'am," Julius said nervously.

"Well, you are a charmer, honey bun! Be careful! The other kids will tease you if they think you're the teacher's pet!" she said with a wink and a smile before directing him towards a desk in the front of class.

After Mrs. Gray made sure that there were no more students, she closed the door and walked to the blackboard. "Hello, children. My name is Mrs. Gray, and I have been teaching for two years. I have one daughter, and I am divorced. Now, I want each of you to tell me your name and a little about yourself."

Slowly, each student began to stand and tell small sketchy things about themselves. When it was his turn, Julius was nervous, but Mrs. Gray smiling at him made him feel better.

After him came Angelica Gray. She looked like a childhood version of their teacher, so it didn't take a rocket scientist to figure out that Angelica was Mrs. Gray's daughter.

Julius was infatuated with Angelica. She was caramel brown, with very light hazel eyes, and had long, flowing wavy hair. She wore a red T-shirt with Minnie Mouse on it, a red and black plaid skirt, and her shoes matched her shirt. Angelica dressed like they were rich. Yes sir, Julius was in love, and by lunch he wanted to marry Angelica and spend the rest of his life with her.

At lunch he sat alone because most of the kids knew each other and had their own little cliques.

Angelica walked up behind him and asked if she could sit with him. He was more than happy; he was ecstatic! "Yeah! Uh, I mean, I don't care," Julius said.

She talked a lot, but he didn't mind. She told him that everyone calls her "Jelly", so he should too. She asked about his family, how he liked Texas, what his favorite games were, what his favorite food was, and if he had a bike. Julius had never answered so many questions in his whole life.

By the time he went back to class, she was the only girl for him in his mind.

Chapter 8

New Kid on the Block

Kenny Waters was a mean fourth grader that was as dumb as a turkey and as strong as an ox, probably because he had been held back twice and was supposed to be in sixth grade. He was in love with Angelica Gray, and any boy seen talking to her was immediately the enemy. It didn't matter who it was, and with Julius being the new kid it only made it worse.

"Hey, nigga, get away from my girl!" Kenny said.

"I am not your girlfriend, Kenny!" Angelica snarled.

Julius was still trying to figure out what was going on when Kenny hit him as hard as he could, and to Kenny's amazement Julius didn't fall down. Julius was in pain and he was scared but, he was more angry than scared.

"Fight! Fight! Fight!" he could hear the other kids on the playground chanting louder and louder.

He didn't want to fight, but he had to.

Mrs. Gray was coming to call her class in from recess when she noticed two boys squared off. "Break this nonsense up, boys! Kenny Waters, if you tried as hard to be smart as you do to be a bully, you'd be in college already!" she barked.

Julius looked around and noticed about twenty or so boys ranging from ages seven to twelve, watching very closely. Although they all looked different, they all held one common thread; they all had blue bandanas hanging from their left back pockets.

Jelly noticed him looking and said, "All those boys are from Dixon Circle. They're in a gang."

Julius knew about gangs. In his old neighborhood in Michigan, the Disciples were always fighting the Vice Lords, and his older brother, Kolby was a Disciple so gangs were nothing new to him. He was still angry though, because Kenny had embarrassed him, and his attitude wouldn't let him forgive or forget.

Once back in class, time seemed to creep by slowly, and then it slowed to a crawl. Julius was calculating how he would get even with Kenny Waters, and it was going to be nothing nice.

Three o'clock finally rolled around and the school bell rang. As far as Julius was concerned, that bell might as well be the bell in the boxing ring. He saw Kenny from a distance, dropped his book bag and took off running towards him, slowly at first, and then faster. He knew that if he timed it right, the impact would shake Kenny and the surprise would confuse him.

He plowed into Kenny like a football player and Kenny hit the ground, dazed and confused. He didn't know what or who had hit him or what they were hitting him for. Nobody had ever challenged Kenny before, so this was new to him. His eye hurt and he tasted blood... his blood. Kenny started to cry, not from pain, but mostly from embarrassment because all of the kids were laughing and cheering for the new kid.

Kenny couldn't get up. He could only curl up in a ball and beg Julius to stop, but Julius wouldn't.

Then abruptly, the punches stopped. He looked up and, *"Bam!"* He felt a shoe hit him in his face. When he woke up, Mr. Bradley, the Youth Action Counselor was standing over him.

"Well, well, well, Mr. Waters! You finally met your match, huh? I told you, you've got to bring ass to get ass, and you, my young friend, got your ass whipped today!"

"Whatever, Mr. B! That lil' nigga stole me!" Kenny whined.

"Whatever he did, he whooped your ass!" the older man chuckled.

All the kids standing around applauded as Julius walked to his locker. Some called him a hero, and some called him "super nigga". He didn't think it was funny. He didn't want Jelly thinking that he was a troublemaker or a bad person. But some things had to be done.

He was almost at the front exit when one of the boys with the blue bandanas came up to him and said, "Hey, cuzz. Duddy wanna talk to you."

They walked outside, and there stood Duddy, an 8th grader. He had on blue Dickie pants, a white T-shirt, blue Chuck Taylors and a blue bandana in his left back pocket. "Say, lil' homie. I heard you rode on dat mark, Kenny, cuzz."

Julius didn't really understand the slang, so he just looked at him.

"Cuzz, did you hear the big homie?"

"Huh?" Julius asked.

"He said he heard you whooped Kenny's ass."

"Oh, yeah... I guess," Julius said.

"We're from Dixon Circle, and we claim D.C.G.C. 357um. That's our gang. We're Crips, and you're going to be in our gang," Duddy said.

"I don't think so!" Big Julius said. He had been listening as he walked up. "Junior, get in the car! Look, you little thugs! Stay away from my son before I give your mammy's something to dress up for!"

"Yes sir!" Duddy stated.

As big Julius walked away he thought to himself, *Damn! A gang banger with manners!* "So, you were at school fighting, huh?" he asked his son.

"Daddy, he hit me first," Lil' Julius explained.

"Did you win? Well, no need to ask that, because you rode on that mark, Kenny cuzz!" Big Julius, said mimicking Duddy. They both laughed. "So, how was your first day?"

"It was good. My teacher's name is Mrs. Gray, and she's pretty and nice, and..."

While his son recounted his day, Julius Sr.'s mind wandered. Sometimes when he talked to his son, he forgot how young the boy was because he was so smart. But at times like this when he went on and on about something he liked, it made him remember that his lil' man was only eight.

They pulled up to a house that Lil' Julius had never seen before. It was big... bigger than the house in Michigan. It was beige with a screened in porch that went around the entire house, and had grass in the front yard that was full and green. He sat in the car looking out of the window and wondering whose house this was, when his father broke into his thoughts.

"Junior, come walk with me, mane."

"'K," Julius replied.

They walked around the front of the house, then the side and then the back. Julius noticed two massive pecan trees in the back yard and a swing set, so whoever lived there obviously had kids. He was getting a little sad, because he loved his aunt and uncle, but he wanted his own house.

Julius Sr. noticed his son getting irritated and asked, "Do you like this house, little man?"

"Uh-huh! It's big!" They walked to the front in silence, and with tears welling up in his eyes the boy said, "Daddy?"

"Yeah, Junior?"

"I want to go home now."

His father gave a faint laugh, pulled a set of keys from his pocket and said, "You are home, baby boy."

Julius had been hoping for his own house, and now maybe he could make friends and have some more kids to walk to school with.

They walked inside the house, and before he could get a good look around his father picked him up and carried him upstairs to his own room. It was decked out with G.I. Joe sheets, curtains and pillow cases. He even had his own bathroom.

Big Julius beamed with happiness at seeing the obvious joy on his son's face. He sat him down and explained to him that he wanted it to be a surprise. He wanted him to always remember that hard work paid off, whether good or bad, and to always strive for good, because even though bad paid, it was not worth it.

The youngster nodded his head in agreement, even though he wasn't absolutely sure why his father was telling him this. He knew it must have been important, because his father had his "Daddy face" on; that stern face that said "I am not playing".

"Do you understand what I mean?" Big Julius asked.

"I think so, Daddy."

"Well, let me also tell you this, son." He knelt down, put his hands on each side of his sons face and told him in a slow measured tone, "Baby boy, never be ashamed of what you do. But whatever you do, be the best at it. If you want to be a doctor, be the best doctor you can. If you want to be a thief, be the best thief you can. If you decide to be a killer, be the most efficient killer you can be. But always remember that in doing wrong, the consequences always outweigh the benefits. Be thorough in your dealings, and always be a man of your word." With that being said, he picked his son up into his arms and held him close in an almost bear hug.

"I love you, Daddy," the little boy said

"I love you more, lil' man… believe that."

With Julius Jr.'s new home came a renewed sense of worth and a boost in self-esteem. He thought that they were rich now because everything in the house was brand new. He had heard his Uncle Charlie call his daddy "Nigga rich," and his daddy had laughed that big manly laugh and replied, "Act as if!" So even if they weren't rich, Julius Jr. was going to act as if.

That night as he ironed his clothes for school he made sure to pay extra attention to the creases, lining up his seams perfectly. He even decided to use a little starch. He wanted to make sure Mrs. Gray noticed him tomorrow. He scrubbed his sneakers, washed his shoe strings, ironed his shirt so the collar was even, and he even ironed his socks.

He stripped down to his Fruit of the Loom's and was making faces and posing in the mirror on his door like the wrestlers did, when Big Ju walked in. "What 'cha doing, killa?" his father laughed.

"Nothing, Daddy," he responded, obviously embarrassed.

"Well listen, Jr. I'm stepping out for a minute and I should be back in an hour or so. Don't go outside and keep these doors locked. You hear me?"

"Yes, Daddy

After his father left, Julius went downstairs and ate dinner in front of the 27" floor model console TV with the stereo on top. *Yes sir, we are rich!* he thought. *Man, we're living like Arnold and Willis from my favorite show, "Different Strokes"!*

His father had made meatloaf, mashed potatoes, butter beans with bacon, and corn bread. And to top it off, he had grape Kool-Aid to drink. It seemed to him that he had inhaled the food, because as soon as he sat down it was gone.

He wanted more, but his father always told him to eat to live, not live to eat. So, he decided to take a bath and get ready for bed. *Tomorrow will be a good day,* he decided.

As soon as his head touched the pillow, he was asleep.

Chapter 9

Always on Time

Julius came into the house in a pretty good mood until he walked into the kitchen and noticed his son had taken the liberty to eat, but wasn't courteous enough to wash the dishes and put away the food. He just ate and hauled ass. He stopped, took another quick look around and thought, *How can I teach him responsibility if I let him get away with shit like this?*

He marched up the stairs two at a time until he reached his son's door, walked right in, snatched the covers off of him and said sternly, "Get up! Go downstairs and clean up your mess! You ain't got no maid service, boy!"

Lil' Ju wiped the sleep from his eyes and headed for the kitchen. The tone in his father's voice told him that now wasn't the time to dispute his wishes or pout about it. *Why couldn't I just wash them tomorrow after school?* he thought. *Oh well! What was done was done. I'll finish and try to hurry up and get back to sleep.*

Big Ju marveled at how his son was taking it like a big boy. But then again, that was his pride and joy; his "little twin" from looks to attitude. Everybody said so, and everybody couldn't be wrong.

The next day, Lil' Ju was up early and getting dressed when his father came into his room to wake him for school. His father only smiled and told him, "Don't forget to brush your teeth."

As Lil' Ju was walking to school and feeling on top of the world, a group of kids across the street on their way to school invited him to walk with them. He was happy to accompany them, and even as they talked he was still in his own world.

"What's up, mane?" a husky kid asked. "I'm BB, this is Ray, this is Shuntae, and Keisha," BB said as he pointed each kid out to Lil' Ju. Shuntae and Keisha were twin girls about his age. "And this is my little brother, Boo. Where you from, mane?"

Ju looked at the older boy, and with no hesitation he mimicked his accent and said, "I'm from Michigan, mane."

They all chuckled as they reached the school yard.

Out of the corner of his eye, Julius noticed Duddy and the rest of his gang watching him. As he got closer to the door they moved towards him.

"Hey, lil' homie. How you doing?"

"I'm okay, I guess," Ju responded.

Duddy laughed a little and shook his head, and nodded towards Ju's newfound friends. "I see you made friends with some of the BG's." BG's were "baby gangsters" in South Dallas. They were a part of the gang but considered too young to really put in work. Now Julius got nervous, because the first friends he really made would piss his father off because he didn't want him hanging with those kinds of kids.

When Julius walked into school, the first person he saw was Angelica. He couldn't stop staring at her. *Damn, she's so pretty! And she always dresses so nice,* he thought. She had on a yellow shirt with Tweety Bird on the front of it, dark blue Jordache jeans, yellow and white tennis shoes, and to top it off, she had yellow and white ribbons in her hair. Julius didn't know who he loved more; her or her mother. Yes sir, he would fight Kenny Waters every day if he had to.

He snapped out of his daydream to see Angelica, Tonya, Mimi and Raquel staring at him and giggling.

The bell had already rang and he was late. Angelica lingered in the hallway and held the door open for him as if to tell him to hurry up.

Julius scurried past her, and just as he was about to take his seat, Mrs. Gray called him and Angelica to the hallway.

"Julius you're a very bright and gifted young man, but..." she let that "but" linger for emphasis. "But, if you ever intend to use the beautiful mind that God blessed you with, you have to be responsible, and with responsibility comes the wisdom to know that punctuality is a key ingredient to success! Angelica, I realize that you were only trying to help, but you too must learn when helping someone goes too far. Self- preservation is the key, and in trying to help Julius you in turn made yourself late. You will not be shown favor because you are my daughter. Therefore, you will both stay after school and help me grade papers and clean the classroom."

They could only muster faint "Yes ma'am's" as they hung their heads and headed to their desks.

The day seemed to drag by, but Julius didn't mind, because after school he would be alone with Angelica and Mrs. Gray. He had to make it quick though, because his father didn't like him to be late for dinner. He always said that a family that ate together stayed together. He knew his father would be a little upset, but he was willing to pay that price for the beautiful hour he was about to spend with "his" Angelica.

Chapter 10

Change is Gon' Come

Big Julius had a lot on his mind and a lot on his plate. He was starting to feel like a flunky. He knew all of the same people and all the same connects as Booty Green and his boys Rabbit and Yellow Shoes did. The way Julius saw it, why should he and Charlie Boy keep making these dudes money instead for themselves?

Julius called Charlie. "Hey, baby bro, I need you to come to my crib when you get a chance. I want to discuss some shit with you."

Charlie listened for any sounds of distress or urgency in his brother's voice, and he heard none. "Alright, Julius, man. Gimme a lil' bit of time and I'll be right over."

******

Charlie Boy rolled a joint and sat down at the kitchen table to speak with Pearl and have a cup of coffee with just a little sugar and milk, the way he liked it.

Pearl looked at her husband with respect, love and total loyalty. She knew from experience in dealing with her husband that his wheels were turning. He was there with her physically, but mentally he was far away. "What did Julius say, baby?" she asked him.

"He didn't say too much really. Just that he wants me to come by, which leads me to believe that it's about business since he didn't want to talk over the phone, you know?"

Pearl pulled up a chair and sat in front of him and cradled his head in her hands. "Charlie Gage, I love you, and I know in my heart of hearts that your brother would never put you in danger. You two just be careful whatever the situation. Baby, please promise me."

Charlie just smiled. Pearl worried about him every time he left the house. Even though she had good reason to worry, he still tried to comfort her and reassure her. There were some snake ass people out there. Charlie knew it and Pearl knew it, so he didn't try to play her like everything was peachy keen. "I promise, Pearly baby. Now, I'ma take a shower and throw some clothes on so that I can get over there and see what's going on."

And with that being said, Charlie headed upstairs to shower.

******

Julius made himself a cup of coffee and sat down to read the *Dallas Morning News*. As he read, he thought to himself that it seems like if it's not bad news, it's not news at all.

Julius Jr. was in the living room watching Saturday morning cartoons while eating a bowl of Cookie Crisp cereal. Julius Sr. could tell that the little man had been digging in the box for the prize, because there were little cookie crumbs all over the countertop.

By the time Charlie Boy arrived, Julius was on his third cup of coffee.

Charlie came through the door and scooped his nephew up. "What's up, Nephew? How's Unc's favorite nephew?" he asked and kissed Julius Jr. on the cheek.

Lil' Julius winced. He hated it when his Uncle Charlie treated him like a baby. "I'm fine, Uncle Charlie. 'He-Man' is on." That was his way of letting his uncle know that he was interrupting his cartoons.

"Okay, Nephew. Sorry to disturb your 'He-e-e-e-e-Man' cartoon!" Charlie said jokingly.

Julius was still seated and reading the paper when Charlie came into the dining room. "What's up, big brother? My nephew just brushed me off for his cartoons!" Charlie said laughing.

"Yeah, mane, when little man is into his cartoons, he doesn't wanna hear or see nothing else, which is kinda good because he won't be disturbing us while we talk," Julius said. He looked at his little brother closely. He knew that what he was going to propose to him was dangerous and deadly, but it was necessary for them to have financial stability. "Charles, man, we been hustling for these niggas, running the club, and even though we are making money, we aren't making nearly enough," Julius began.

The only time Julius called Charlie "Charles" is when he was deadly serious.

Julius continued. "Man, the way I see it, there is enough money out here for all of us. If they can't stand a little competition, then they don't need to be in business."

"Julius, the quickest way to start a war is to put your hands in a man's pockets. I'm down for whatever, but let's go into this realistically and with our eyes wide open. You know as well as I do that it could lead to bloodshed," Charlie said in a whisper.

"I'm fully aware of what's coming, bruh, trust me. I'm also aware that even though we have made beaucoup money, there's more of it out there, and I am not trying to work for anybody else when the opportunity for us to own our own shit is possible!" Julius huffed.

"Calm down, player! I'm your brother, and I'm with you one-hundred percent. Why don't we step to them niggas and let 'em know that we're striking out on our own so it doesn't look like we are trying to be shady?" Charlie suggested, even though he knew the reaction it would spark.

"Nigga, I don't need Booty Green, Rabbit or Yellow Shoes' muthafuckin' permission to do a got-damn thang! Charlie Boy, if I had my way I'd just as soon spill them niggas' blood than negotiate with them!" Julius spat.

"Julius, man, it's not about negotiating, it's about the code in the streets. We've made some damn good money with these cats."

"Naw, we made damn good money *for* these cats!" Julius interjected.

Charlie continued, "Okay, *with* them, *for* them... whatever. The point is that we've made some good money, and even though I'm with you, I don't want our moves to be taken the wrong way, because the niggas we cater to are the same cutthroat niggas that follow the code, you know?" Charlie explained.

Julius just looked at his brother. He knew that Charlie wasn't scared, but to Julius, he always over-analyzed shit too much. Julius' plan was simple: Booty Green and his boys depended largely on the gamblers in his afterhours spots to move his bootleg liquor. Dallas stopped selling liquor at midnight, but the streets stayed thirsty.

Julius and Charlie would concentrate on two businesses to increase the cash flow. They would set up bootleg houses on each end of South Dallas so that all of their houses would serve the major neighborhoods in there. Bon-Ton, Pine and Colonial, Park Row, Bank Street, Dixon Circle and Second Ave. would all be covered. In these houses they would sell liquor, beer, wine and weed.

After he explained all of this to Charlie, his little brother was on board with it. Charlie still knew that it would cause bloodshed and so did Julius, but he thought of profits coming to them was too great.

Julius would go along with his little brother's suggestion and talk to Booty Green about striking out on their own. If he didn't like it, Julius and Charlie would do it anyway. Julius knew the dangers of taking food out of a man's mouth. He also knew the dangers of outliving your usefulness to a person you were making money for.

Julius and Charlie dropped off Lil' Julius with Pearl. From there they headed to the Bus Stop Lounge to meet with Booty Green and Rabbit. There really wouldn't be much to talk about. They were just going to keep it simple and explain to them what they were going to do.

It was just before dark when they arrived at the lounge, and people had already started to file in. Saturday nights was always busy, which was perfect due to the fact that Booty Green was dangerous, but he wasn't a fool. He wouldn't start a gunfight in his place of business.

The brothers waded through the crowd to the office in the rear where Booty Green and Rabbit were waiting. Charlie knocked on the door to the office and a pretty petite white lady with blonde hair and a dark tan opened the door. She gave Charlie and Julius a quaint smile and closed the door behind them. She was a new waitress at the Bus Stop Lounge, and one of Yellow Shoes' best girls. But she was pregnant so she was off limits for a little while. But as it stood, she still had her figure and girlish good looks.

"Come on in, fellas. What's your flavor?" Booty Green asked.

Julius said flatly, "This ain't no social call, homeboy, this about business."

Booty Green looked at Julius like he wanted to kill him, but just as quickly as he got angry his features softened and he was calm again. "Okay, player, slow your roll! Felicia baby, that'll be all for right now," he said, dismissing the white woman before turning back to Julius. "Okay, mane, now what's so urgent that it's got you being disrespectful and shit, bruh?"

"I'm not being disrespectful, mane. I just don't have time to exchange niceties. I just came through to give you a little courtesy call," Julius stated.

Booty Green looked at Rabbit, and then looked at Julius and Charlie with a murderous smirk and said coldly, "Really? Extend me a courtesy, huh? And what exactly would this courtesy consist of?"

Charlie looked irritated as he began to speak. "Me and my brother just wanted to come through and put you up on game. We intend to strike out and do our own thang in this business. We just came by to let you know as a courtesy, ya dig?"

"Oh, I dig! And what exactly is this business y'all are so gung-ho about jumping into?" Green asked.

"We're planning on doing some bootlegging," Julius said, obviously irritated "We didn't come to get your permission, nigga; we just came to give you the game. Muthafuckas ain't tryna work for you forever, mane!" Julius exclaimed

Rabbit started laughing almost uncontrollably, and then looked at Green and said, "Damn, Booty Green! You got your workers coming up in this muthafucka talking to you like you're a real lame, mane!"

Rabbit's teasing only made Booty Green's blood boil even more. He ignored him and poured himself a Hennessey and Coke. He stood there stirring his drink and casually asked, "And what am I supposed to be doing while you muthafuckas are taking money out of my pocket and food off my plate?"

Julius was getting pissed. To him, Booty Green was a disrespectful, whiney little punk. But that wouldn't stop him from getting his money. Booty Green had served as the unofficial king of South Dallas for far too long, and it was time for somebody to take him off of his high horse and give him some competition.

"Nigga, we're grown ass men, and you don't own this fucking city! We are done!" Charlie spat.

Julius had to smile inside. His little brother handled that like he would have handled it.

"Okay, man, you're right... you're right. But this shit ain't over! Got-dammit, fuck you Gage niggas!" Booty Green said angrily.

With that being said, Julius and Charlie turned to leave. In Julius' mind he already knew what needed to be done. Booty Green was beside himself, and Julius knew that he would never let it rest. South Dallas was cutthroat; an entire neighborhood known for its dog eat dog attitude.

Chapter 11

Killa Talk

Big Julius wasn't in very good spirits today. In his mind Booty Green and Rabbit had crossed him for the last time. Charlie tried calming him down but he wasn't hearing it. "Charlie, listen. All a man has is his balls and his word. And if a nigga ain't honorable enough to live up to his word, then fuck him!"

Charlie knew better than to dispute his brother when he was like this. His only option was to try and defuse the situation with reason. "Ju, I understand that you're upset, but think about your junior, mane."

Julius looked at his little brother, and for a split second he thought he saw fear cross his face. But he quickly dismissed it. Charlie wasn't afraid of shit. He was the brother that was most like him. But with rage and venom seething from every word, he stated bluntly, "Nigga, fuck that! I *am* thinking about my baby! That's why I need my muthafuckin' money! I told both of those fools what would happen if they played with my bread, didn't I? Didn't I?" he asked more firmly, as if to permanently burn it into Charlie's brain. "My son will not go without because those bastards wanna play with my money!"

"Okay, bruh," Charlie said flatly. "You know I'ma back whatever play you throw out."

Julius knew that his little brother meant what he said. He didn't start trouble, but Charlie was known for finishing it.

"You know what you need, Julius?" Charlie asked.

Julius could see a smirk on Charlie's face, letting him know that there were no hard feelings. "Okay, I'll play the game. What is it that I need, Charlie Boy, huh?

"You need some pussy! Maybe your ass wouldn't be so damn mean!"

They both laughed, but even as Julius laughed he had an eerie feeling in the pit of his stomach. He had always been extra careful, but something was wrong. Rabbit and Green were mean dudes, and even though he felt stronger and more ruthless he couldn't shake the feeling of dread. He had made plenty of money and he could afford to let this slide, but if he let it slide he would never be safe, nor would his family, especially his youngest son. His mind was made up; he would handle the situation with swift and harsh vengeance.

He went home, and as soon as he walked into his house he decided that now was as good a time as any to pray, and pray he did… hard! He asked God first to care for his son; secondly, he asked for protection against his enemies; and lastly, he prayed for forgiveness for what he was about to do.

He checked the house, and then went to his closet to check on his safe. His money was intact. He pushed a button inside the safe and a panel inside his closet slid open, revealing an arsenal of weapons ranging from small caliber pistols to machine guns. He took out a few guns and loaded them into a duffel bag.

He then called Charlie and Pearl and asked them to care for Lil' Julius until things were safe. Charlie wanted to go with his brother, but he knew arguing would be pointless.

Julius picked out black socks, black shoes, a black turtleneck and black gloves, laid them out on the bed and started the shower. He took a very long, slow shower, mainly because his mind was working a mile a minute. He almost allowed the "what ifs" to creep in, but he dismissed them just as quickly.

Once out of the shower he shaved and splashed on his favorite Pierre Cardin cologne, got dressed, and loaded his guns and the rest of his tools of the trade into his car.

He drove to all of the hot spots looking for Rabbit and Green. He drove down Pine Street to the R.C. Lounge, he went to the Bus Stop Lounge, he went to the 2nd Avenue Pool Hall, and he went to Lady Love II strip club. Julius rode for hours through the streets of South Dallas to no avail. There was no sign of them.

Julius caught a glimpse of headlights in his rearview mirror but dismissed it. He drove home kind of pissed because he really wanted to get rid of his "little problem".

Once at home he sat in the driveway for a while just thinking. Something he couldn't shake was a Bible verse he had heard:

"Vengeance is mine, sayeth the Lord."

It kept playing over and over in his head.

He made his way to the front door and put his key into the lock. He had the thought that maybe he should take his son and his money and leave town, but he couldn't. His pride wouldn't let him. He was tired of running.

He turned the key and walked inside, and there sitting in the dark he could see two figures. He reached for his pistol but realized he'd left it in the car.

Rabbit spoke. "Come in and sit down, nigga. We need to talk.

Julius Sr. was seething with anger because they were in his house, but even more so because he had slipped and left his gun in his car. He moved to turn on a light, but a third man knocked him to the ground.

"No need for lights, nigga. The only light you're gonna see is gonna be at the end of that long dark tunnel, muthafucka!" Rabbit exclaimed.

Green stood up and stared at Julius as if to study him. It was a shame he had to kill him, because he had always liked Julius. But he knew from experience that if he didn't kill him, Julius would not hesitate to kill him and all that he loved. Green said in a measured tone, "Julius, listen. It didn't have to come to this, mane. You just can't let shit go. I for one never wanted shit to come to this, but you're a disrespectful and ungrateful muthafucka. I put food on your table, clothes on your fucking back, and this is how you repay me, nigga?"

Julius' mind was racing. How did they know what he was planning to do so quickly? Better yet, who had crossed him? There was only Charlie Boy, Pearl, and Pearls friend, Chele. It had to be Chele. That bitch was bitter because he had turned her down. She had to be the one. *Bitch!* he fumed.

Green continued. "You think you're gonna waltz yo' country ass up in South Dallas and do shit yo' way? Muthafucker, I *own* South Dallas, from Bon Ton to Pine, from Colonial to Park Row, from Bank Street to Dixon Circle. Bitch, don't nothing happen in this shit hole without Booty Green and Rabbit knowing about it. Your fucking mouth just signed your death certificate, nigga!"

Julius wasn't going out like a bitch. He looked at Green and stated flatly, "Nigga, if you think I'ma beg you like a lil' bitch, you're crazy as a mother fucker!" He lunged at Green, barely missing him before he heard the first shot, and then felt the burning.

A second shot rang out, and Julius felt numbness in his back. He was still fighting and clawing, trying to stay alive. He managed to get a grip on a third unknown man's leg, and then it became clear. There was only one nigga in Dallas that wore yellow snake skin boots; Yellow Shoes the pimp. Then the third shot rang out and everything went black.

Yellow Shoes kicked Julius' hands away from his shoes. He, Green and Rabbit stood around Julius' crumpled body, talking shit and taunting the dead man.

Rabbit stared at the men he had just committed murder with and started laughing hysterically. "Yellow Shoes, I know you a stomp-down pimp, and Charlie Boy taking Pearl didn't set well with you, but why Julius? I mean, me and Green was gonna get him anyway, but why did you want him dead?"

Yellow Shoes thought for a moment, then smirked and said coldly, "'Cause with this black muthafucka gone, his brother is a dead man. Plus, I ain't never liked the smut ass nigga anyways."

"Man, I hear sirens! Let's go!" Green said.

"We'll all go out the back in different directions. And you niggas keep y'alls' muthafuckin' mouths closed. Dead men can't talk, and I ain't telling on myself, agreed?"

Rabbit and Yellow Shoes both agreed, and they parted ways into the night.

Chapter 12

Hate On

Big Julius awoke in Parkland Hospital. He couldn't move and his head hurt. He tried to talk to a nearby nurse but when he opened his mouth nothing came out. He looked to his left and he saw Pearl crying. He looked to his right and saw Charlie holding Lil' Julius. Charlie was also holding Julius' hand, and when Julius squeezed his brother's hand he jumped.

"Man, how you feeling?" Charlie asked.

Julius made a motion with his hands like he was thirsty. Charlie went to get the nurse, and she came over with a cup of water and a straw.

After taking a few sips, Julius cleared his throat and began to speak in a slow, labored tone. "Charlie, listen. I don't think I'm going to make it, bro, but before I go, I need you to know some things. Those niggas thought I was dead, man, and they thought nobody would ever find out what they'd done to me. It was Rabbit, Booty Green and Yellow Shoes…" Julius coughed.

"*Yellow Shoes?*" Charlie screamed.

"Yeah, Yellow Shoes. He got involved 'because he wants to hurt you about Pearl, bro. Charlie, protect my boy with your life man. Promise me!"

Charlie choked back tears and said quietly, "I got you, mane."

"Naw…" Julius coughed. "Promise me, man. Please!"

"I promise on my life, mane. I got my nephew," Charlie said, and began to cry.

Lil' Julius walked over and asked if everything was okay, and his father shook his head no. He told his brother to let him speak to his son alone.

When they were alone, Julius looked into his son's eyes and had to choke back tears. *My baby!* he thought. *So full of promise, and so much like me.* "Baby boy, listen," Julius began. "I have a lot to say and a short time to say it in, so listen to Daddy closely. I want you to soak up everything that I say. Baby, Daddy might not be around to much longer, but I want you to know that I love you very much. I always have and always will. You're my reason for breathing, my reason for fighting and the reason that I did a lot of the things I did."

He paused to take a breath. "I only wanted the best for you, son, and that led to some unwise decisions in my life. But I made them knowing that if they played out, you would be set. There are things in my safe at home for you, which you will need when you're older. But only use them when you need them. Be strong, but be humble, son. Know and acknowledge God in all you do. That's most important. Your word is your bond. If you speak it, mean it!"

Big Julius paused and took a sip of water to allow his words to soak into his sons mind. "Always strive to be your best. If you choose to be a thief, be the best thief. If you decide to be a doctor, be the best doctor. You are a killer's son, baby. And you will learn that your father passed on all of his genes to you… even my killer's genes. Be a good man, son, always, and never ever, ever in your life hit a woman. A woman is your queen, and she is to be cherished as such. If shit gets bad enough for her to take you to your dark place, you leave, do you hear me?" Big Julius asked. It was obvious that he was in pain.

"Yes, Daddy," the little one said.

His father continued. "You don't have friends, you have associates. Never put too much stock in friendships 'cause people will let you down at every turn. Always look a man in the eyes and give a firm handshake. Don't try to be me, baby; be better than me. And don't be a follower, be a leader. If you're not running it, you are not in it." He coughed a violent cough and went silent.

The doctors came running in and pushed Lil' Julius out of the room before he could say goodbye. He knew in his heart that his father was gone; he could feel it. It felt like someone had ripped his heart out through his chest. He cried to himself, afraid to let his Uncle Charlie see him cry. And also ashamed to let Auntie Pearl see him cry. But silently he cried, silently he wept, and silently he began to feel hatred growing inside of him, but he didn't know for whom. He was just angry that his Daddy was gone, and he missed him already.

Chapter 13

Bastard Life

Charlie sat silently in the corner, still unable to believe that his oldest brother was dead. He looked at the door leading to his brother's room and saw the doctors wheeling him out on a stretcher. He saw Pearl cradling Julius Jr. in her arms, and he was glad that she had turned him away from the door.

So many things were racing through Charlie's mind. *Why had they killed him? What would he tell his nephew? How would he exact his revenge? Where should he go from here?* The questions kept creeping into his head until it gave him a massive headache. His head ached so badly that he felt he might pass out.

Out of all of the brothers, he and Julius had been the closest. He had learned so much from him, and now he was on his own. For a split second he allowed fear and uncertainty to wash over him. Then he began to sob, quietly but steadily. *I have to get my shit together!* Charlie thought.

As suddenly as his fear and sorrow had come on, it was gone. Now he sat silently brooding, angry at himself and feeling that he had somehow let his brother down, and that had cost him his life. He sat thinking long and hard: *How could those niggas have gotten to my brother so quickly?*

******

Pearl brought Charlie his morning paper and cup of coffee. She stood there looking at her husband. He looked worried and tired. She really didn't know what to say to him. She knew how much Julius had meant to Charlie, but she also knew that her husband's pride and temper wouldn't let this go. For the first time since they had been married, she felt afraid and insecure. "Here's your paper and coffee, sweetie," she said with a shaky voice.

Charlie took notice and asked, "What's wrong, baby? Is everything okay?"

Pearl thought about telling him a lie, but he always knew when she was lying. "No, baby, everything isn't okay. I'm scared, Charlie... scared of what could happen to you, and scared of what could happen to me and Ju-Ju Bean."

Charlie's blood ran cold. He was angry at Pearl for believing that he would ever put her and his nephew in danger. "Pearlie baby, listen. I got this shit under control. I would never put you and my nephew in any danger, believe that." He thought for a second then added, "If them niggas wanted me dead, I would be dead already."

Pearl began to cry. "Let's just leave, Charlie. We got money. Let's just leave!" She started to cry uncontrollably.

The sobs were shaking her body and Charlie could sense her fears. He had never seen Pearl like this before. "Pearl, listen, sweets. I'm never going to do anything to

78

jeopardize this family or my wellbeing, but I can't let this go! Those muthafuckas killed my brother, and they're going to pay!"

Pearl began to protest, but he quieted her with a wave of his hand. She knew that he was serious... deadly serious.

Charlie had a lot on his mind. He didn't know exactly where to start, but what he did know was who he would start with. That bitch, Chele had to pay.

He sat in his chair contemplating, planning, plotting and strategizing. He would make Chele pay for setting his brother up. It would be harsh and lethal and, by no means would it be quick.

He knew Chele's schedule. Every night she was at the R.C. Lounge until 11 p.m., but on Fridays she would always stay late, hoping to catch one of the high rollers that gambled in the back of the lounge.

Charlie put on his nicest leisure suit that night; black linen with pleats, black Pierre Cardin slippers, a Pierre Cardin belt and a black Dobbs hat. To top it off, he put on his new Cazal black rimmed shades that Pearl had bought him.

He went into the basement and pulled the bookshelf from the wall. Behind it was a small door. He pulled a necklace from inside his shirt with a gold skeleton key on it and used it to unlock the door to his favorite room. In this room he kept all his guns, his money, and his valuable possessions. He had managed to save about $275,000 and had amassed about 30 guns. Between his jewelry and Pearl's jewelry, he was looking at another $200,000.

He grabbed $5,000 from a table stacked with money. He also grabbed twin nickel plated pearl handled .45 caliber handguns that his brother had given him for his birthday some years back.

He locked up the room, replaced the bookshelf and turned to go up the stairs, and was startled to see Julius Jr. standing at the top of the stairs in his pajamas and with his thumb in his mouth. "What are you doin' up, Junior?" he asked his nephew.

Julius just shrugged his shoulders. He didn't talk much since his father had been killed; just enough to get his point across.

Charlie found it kind of spooky, but he understood. He would hear Julius talking to his father sometimes, as if he was still alive, but he never interrupted because the doctors had told him that his behavior was healthy. It was his way of dealing with the grief. "Well, wait for me and I'll walk you to your room."

Julius smiled. Uncle Charlie reminded him of his father, and he liked it when his uncle tucked him into bed because he always put money underneath his pillow.

"Nephew, listen. I don't know what's going on in your head, but I want you to know that I love you and I'm going to always protect you."

Julius managed a weak, "Okay," but he wasn't convinced. Adults always thought kids didn't know what was going on, but Julius had questions. *How would Uncle Charlie protect him when he couldn't protect his Daddy?* But he would keep his questions to himself for now. There would be plenty of time for questions, but for now he was sleepy.

Chapter 14

The Big Payback

Charlie got to the R.C. Lounge around 11 p.m. He went in nodded to a few people and headed past the bar to the gambling room in the back.

In the gambling room, huddled in a corner were Chele, Yellow Shoes and Booty Green. Rabbit was across the room on the opposite side doing his best to put his mack down on a little chocolate girl named Rita.

Charlie walked in, stopped and looked around. When Yellow Shoes and Booty Green saw him, they stopped talking mid-sentence and stared at him.

Yellow Shoes made a motion for Charlie to join them, and Charlie fought back the urge to pull his guns right then and accepted the invitation. *Evidently they don't think I know,* he thought.

"Ay, sorry to hear about your brother. He was a good dude, mane," Booty Green said flatly.

"Yeah, mane, that nigga was a real class act, mane," Yellow Shoes added.

"Yeah, mane, you live by the gun you die by the gun. My brother knew what time it was," Charlie said. He did not want to give them the slightest clue that he knew it was them who killed his brother.

Chele was able to muster a low, "Hey, Charlie."

Charlie looked at her, and her eyes were trained on the floor. "S'up, Chele?" he said, his voice flat and emotionless.

Rabbit had come from the other side of the room. He walked up, put his hand on Charlie's shoulder and shook his head. "This shit is a shame, bruh," he said. "Do the laws have any idea who did this bullshit?"

"Naw, man! You know them peckerwoods don't give a fuck bout what happens in South Dallas!" Charlie shouted, barely able to control his anger.

Yellow Shoes said in a slow, calculated tone, "Calm down, baby. We're gon' get the muthafuckas, mane. I'ma put some real street soldiers on finding the bastards that hit your brother, playa."

"Yeah," Booty Green added. "We're gonna get them. Charlie, did Big Ju say anything before he died, mane?"

Charlie thought carefully, and knew that he was being tested. He then answered, "Naw, mane. He was already dead when I got there."

Chele had begun to sweat a little, and everybody noticed.

"Bitch, go freshen up! You're sweating like a Hebrew slave!" Yellow Shoes griped.

Chele flinched at Yellow Shoes' harsh words. "Maybe I should go home and shower and come back," she remarked.

"Yeah, ho, maybe you should!" barked Yellow Shoes.

Chele got up and shuffled towards the doorway. She stopped just short of leaving, looked back and said, "I'm sorry about what happened to Julius, Charlie."

Charlie looked at her, and there was something about the way she said it that touched him. It was like she wasn't sorry he was dead; she was sorry because she had caused it. She had a look of remorse... and fear.

Charlie was mostly known for being laid back, but he was also known to be deadly when crossed, and Chele knew that if he ever found out what she'd done, he wouldn't hesitate to kill her. She walked out into the night, not knowing that tonight would be her last time feeling the crisp Texas breeze.

While Yellow Shoes and the others were talking, Charlie had tuned them out and he was concentrating on how to best get away from them to deal with Chele. She was the first link in a chain that he intended to destroy. "Ay, mane, y'all niggas doin' any gambling tonight?" he asked the trio.

"Yeah, we might shoot some ivory. Why, what's up? You got some money to lose, nigga?" Booty Green asked.

"Yeah, I got a lil' bit of change to make work for me, mane," Charlie said with a laugh. He was known for breaking niggas at dice, so he was sure that they would buy it. "Listen, I only got a C-note on me, so I'ma run home and get some bread. I would have Pearlie bring it, but my nephew's in bed already," he stated.

"Alright, playa, hurry back. I need some of that Gage money!" Rabbit said.

Charlie looked at Rabbit when he made that statement, and felt his blood boil. Those three niggas were jealous of anyone that had more than them, or had the potential to make more.

Chapter 15

Treacherous Bitch

Charlie walked out into the South Dallas night air, surprisingly calm. Chele would be an easy target because she kept the same routine. If she was really going home to shower, she would have candles burning and music blaring.

He got into his car and drove two blocks, and parked in an alley behind her apartment building. He could hear the sound of The Isley Brothers coming from her apartment before he even got out of his car. As he quietly made his way towards the back stairs he passed Blackie, the dope fiend in the driveway, and kept his head down. Besides, Blackie was probably too high to recognize him anyway.

Much to Charlie's surprise, Chele's backdoor was unlocked. As he made his way in quietly, he could hear the shower running from the kitchen where he had come in. It was too damn dark for his taste.

He stood in the doorway of the bathroom seething. He started to just kill her in the shower, but he decided against it. He wanted to talk to her first. He wanted her to know why she was going to die.

Chele stepped out of the shower feeling refreshed. She was thinking that maybe she would move back to Arkansas with her mother and get away until shit cooled down. Yellow Shoes had change a lot since she first meet him and she didn't want to ho for him anymore, plus the nigga was old and couldn't fuck.

Julius was gone, and she was responsible for it. He was the only man that she was actually willing to change for, and he hadn't seen it. And out of anger and embarrassment she had betrayed the only man she had ever really fallen in love with, and she hated herself for it.

Chele saw a shadow move in the corner between the bathroom and front door and went to light another candle to get a better look. She thought it might be Yellow Shoes because she had mistakenly given him a key. When she lit the candle and saw Julius, her heart stopped for a brief second. She squinted to focus her eyes and saw that it wasn't Julius; it was his younger brother, Charlie. "What the fuck are you doing in my crib, Charlie?" she barked.

Charlie just stared at her. The candlelight flickering off of her body gave it an almost angelic glow. She was a fine woman. Every curve seemed so perfect, and her breasts were perfectly round and perky. She was the first woman that Charlie had ever seen with her pussy hair trimmed in the shape of a heart. Her body was perfect, and she was actually a pretty girl. "Sit down, bitch, and listen!" he said calmly.

Chele did as she was told. She was trying hard to remain calm and not show her fear, but it was difficult.

"What do you want, Charlie? I'm not giving you no pussy, because Pearl is my friend," she said nervously.

"Bitch, please! My brother wouldn't fuck you, so why would I? I want your motherfucking soul! Before you die, I want to know why, Chele? Why would you do that to my brother? Better yet, to my nephew? Why are you so muthafucking treacherous?" he asked bluntly.

Chele knew from his hateful words that her time was short, so she might as well come clean. She wanted somebody, anybody to know how she felt. She had tried to tell Pearl, but Pearl had dismissed it as childish flirtation. "Charlie, I'ma be totally honest with you. I know you're going to kill me, and I'm scared, but I want to let you know everything before I die." She began to cry softly, partly out of fear, and partly from pain.

"I loved your brother. I fell in love with him the very first time I saw him. I saw my future with Julius and Julius Jr. I wanted Jr. to love me like he loved Pearly. I was willing to change for Julius, something that I had never considered doing for any other man. I just wanted the chance to show him that I could be a real woman, a chance to show him that I was in his corner."

Chele reached onto the coffee table, grabbed a Benson and Hedges 100 menthol cigarette, lit it, took a deep drag and continued. "I guess I just wanted what you and Pearl had, but Julius only saw me as a ho. And like he used to always say, 'You can't turn a ho into a housewife'. I was always happy to see him, but when I got home every night I would cry and pray to God that he would see how much I cared for him. I felt like he would come around one day, so I started to prepare myself. I talked to my mother about it, and she told me to just let it go and come home. I cried every night, Charlie!"

Chele had begun to sob uncontrollably, but once she had regained her composure she started again. "I let my emotions get the best of me. My shame and sadness gave way to anger and vengeance, so I gave Booty Green and Rabbit information on Julius. If I have to die, at least I will be with him when I get to Heaven. I don't deserve to live, and honestly I don't wanna live without Julius." She sobbed.

Charlie just looked at her in amazement and thought, *This bitch is bananas!* He could tell that she was being sincere, but her feelings went beyond love. Her feelings were psychotic. She was totally obsessed with his brother.

"Charlie, do you mind if I put on a gown or something? I don't want the police to find me like this," she asked.

"Yeah, go ahead but, don't try nothing slick though."

Chele walked to her room in a daze. She felt as though a weight had been lifted off of her shoulders. Her whole life flashed before her eyes. Every lie that she had heard in her life came rushing back at her at once. *Seize the day! Grab the bull by the horns!* All of those things that she had been told were lies.

Chele had poured her heart out to Julius, and he had simply looked at her with pity and coldly turned her down. Her feelings were hurt and her ego was crushed. Over time that hurt had turned to anger, and after that anger had subsided and bitterness had set in. Chele loved Julius but, she hated him for making her feel as though she wasn't good enough. She hated him for not allowing her a chance to prove to him how much she was in love with him.

It was that same bitterness that allowed her to entertain the proposition made by Yellow Shoes, Booty Green and Rabbit. They had essentially made her an offer that was almost impossible to turn down. They wanted her to follow Julius and watch his every move. They wanted to know what time he left home, where he was going, what he was doing when he left, and so on. In turn they would give her $15,000 and a bus ticket to anywhere in the United States that she wanted to go. They convinced her that she could have a fresh start with a wad of cash where nobody knew her name, and that appealed to her greatly. In reality, after Chele had started to think about it she realized that they just wanted her away from Dallas in case anyone started asking questions.

Nothing mattered now though. Charlie knew that she was involved with Julius' murder, and she had accepted the thought of death. She morbidly welcomed it. She had heard stories of the Gage brothers, but more importantly she had heard stories of death. People said that at the moment of death you could see your whole life flash before your eyes.

But this felt different. She could smell death coming. She almost gagged at the sweet putrid smell that she was encountering. She could smell her own withering, rotting flesh. A mix of rotting flesh and wilted flowers seized her nose in a violent concoction of life and death.

She grabbed a silk gown from her dresser drawer and put it on. She also grabbed her snub nosed .38 Special from under her pillow, put it in her mouth and pulled the trigger.

The gunshot startled Charlie. He ran to the room to see Chele crumpled on the floor and bleeding. Half of her brain was splattered on the mirror; the other half was on the floor. He moved quickly, not out of panic, but out of necessity, wiping down everything that he thought he could have possibly touched.

As he moved around the house, a light coming from Chele's second bedroom caught his attention. He walked into the room and gasped. Chele had made up the room like a shrine to Julius. There were candles lit, pictures of Julius everywhere, and stacks and stacks of little love notes all over the floor. He turned off the light and moved towards the door.

He stopped in the kitchen and turned on all the eyes on her gas stove and blew out the flames. He knew that it would take the gas a while to reach the candles, but when it did there would be nobody for the police to find.

Charlie left the apartment after he was sure that nobody was watching. He was halfway down Colonial Boulevard when he heard the explosion. He smiled to himself. "That was too easy," he mused. He reasoned that he hadn't actually killed Chele, so his hands were clean.

Charlie was still basking in his own prowess when he felt cold steel pressed against the back of his neck. He looked through the rearview mirror to see Yellow Shoes in his backseat. The darkness cast a demonic shadow over his mulatto colored skin.

"Nigga, what the fuck did you do to Chele?" Yellow Shoes asked, enraged. "Nigga, make a right on Pine Street. We finna settle this shit right muthafuckin' now!" he barked. He had Charlie drive to a secluded spot in Bon Ton called Rochester Park.

Charlie knew from experience and hearsay that Rochester Park had so many bodies buried in it that the police found it next to impossible to dig them all up. And even with increased patrols of the park, bodies kept piling up. He noticed that they were bypassing the "graveyard" in Rochester Park and were headed towards Turner Court Housing Projects.

Yellow Shoes instructed Charlie to drive to the back of the projects by the railroad tracks.

Turner Court Projects were known to be extremely ruthless, in the sense that they were a close knit community that never talked to outsiders or police. You could literally murder a man on someone's front doorstep, and the resident would swear to the police that they hadn't seen a thing.

"Pull in right here, jive ass nigga!" Yellow Shoes ordered sharply.

Charlie guided his car into a slightly wooded area where he could see flames.

"Get yo' punk ass out the car, muthafucka!"

Charlie could hear the hatred in Yellow Shoes' every word.

Rabbit and Booty Green were standing next to the fire and by what looked like a small grave.

Rabbit began to speak in a rambling fashion, and every word he spoke cut into Charlie like a knife. "Man, you ig'nant just like yo' dumb ass muthafuckin' brother. What you thought, nigga? That we didn't know you knew? You muthafuckin' Gage boys thought y'all was so smart. You know what, boy? It was fun killing yo' punk ass brother, but killing yo' ass is gonna damn near gimme a nut!" he sneered.

Booty Green doused Charlie with gasoline. It blinded him and the fumes made his nose burn.

Rabbit continued his verbal assault. "Nigga, now you can join yo' bitch ass brother in hell! You know what they say: 'Ashes to ashes' and all that good shit!"

Rabbit, Booty Green and Yellow Shoes all laughed.

Charlie's eyes were closed so he never saw Booty Green come up behind him and push him into the grave. All three of the gangsters unloaded their handguns into his body until he was no longer moving. After they were sure he was dead, they took torches and set his body on fire. They watched him burn until his body was no longer able to be recognized. They began to throw dirt into the hole and bragged about finally ridding South Dallas of the Gage boys.

Rabbit mused to himself. "Shit, if Lil' Julius was old enough I'd kill that little muthafucka too, mane!"

What they didn't understand was that even though the projects had sealed lips, its eyes and ears never slept.

Chapter 16

Life is Too Short

Pearl sat on the front porch staring out into the South Dallas night. She knew that something was wrong; she could feel it in her gut. Charlie had told her not to worry, that he would be back shortly, but it was 3 o'clock in the morning. She knew that he was grieving and she wanted to give him his space, but Ju-Ju Bean needed them both. His little heart was broken, and Pearl knew it. This wasn't like Charlie Boy. He loved little Julius and he loved Pearl, so if he was going to be too late he would've stopped and called.

Pearl went inside the house and checked on Julius, who was fast asleep.

The phone rang and it startled her. She didn't realize how jumpy she was. Pearl rushed to the phone, hoping that it was her husband on the other end. "Hello! Hello!" she screamed. She was in no mood for phone pranks. She heard a deep voice and it sent a chill down her spine. The voice was muffled, like someone was intentionally trying to disguise their voice.

"Pearl," the voice said. "Listen and listen close. Julius is dead, Charlie Boy is dead, Chele is dead, and they are coming for Julius Jr. If you know like I know, you'll take your nephew and disappear. The same people that killed Julius killed your husband, so don't think for a second that they won't kill you and your precious nephew."

And then there was silence. They had hung up the phone, and Pearls heart sank. Her biggest fear realized, she let out a piercing scream. She fell to her knees trying to get a grasp on what was going on. *Was Charlie really gone? Would they really try and hurt her and Julius Jr.? Did she really need to leave the home that her husband had made for her?* Her mind was racing a million miles a minute. She didn't know whether it was serious or whether somebody was playing a cruel joke. If they were fucking with her head, she reasoned that Chele would answer the phone.

With shaking hands she dialed Chele's number and her phone just rang and rang. With that, she knew and felt dread in her gut. She knew that Charlie was dead.

And now it was time for her to do what she knew Charlie Boy would want; get her and Julius to safety.

Pearl scurried around the house picking up important items like photos and documents, things of either sentimental value or of measurable importance. She packed quickly and quietly. Her mind was racing, but her thoughts were cloudy and it was hard to think. Shit, it was hard to breathe! Where would she go? She didn't have any family that she could rely on.

She needed to get in contact with Najé to let her know what was going on, and she needed to call the rest of Charlie and Julius' brothers. But first and foremost she had to get her Ju-Ju to safety.

She ran upstairs, woke up Lil' Julius softly and got him dressed. The young boy didn't ask any questions. He didn't say much really because he was too sleepy.

Pearl was working against the clock now. It was already after 4:00 a.m. and she wanted to be away from the Dallas city limits by the time the sun came up. She couldn't shake the nervousness. It was so damn dark outside. She had asked Charlie a long time ago to put some flood lights up. Oh well, it was too late now.

Pearl loaded her Cadillac up and then went back inside to get Lil' Julius. She laid him across the backseat and covered him from head to toe with his blanket. She gave one last look at her home before she got into her Eldorado and drove away. This was her last night in the home that Charles Gage had made for her.

Chapter 17

Slugz and Pearlz

Rabbit, Booty Green and Yellow Shoes sat in Rabbit's den talking about what had happened earlier that night.

Yellow Shoes had a bloodlust. He wanted to eliminate anybody that had any connection to Julius and Charlie Boy. That meant Pearl had to die, and that meant Julius Jr. had to die, and die they would if he had anything to do with it. "Man, the last thang I wanna do is to be looking over my muthafuckin' shoulder, waiting for this little bastard to grow up, learn the truth and come after me!" Yellow Shoes screamed.

To the other two men he seemed paranoid, and that could be dangerous.

Rabbit started to speak, but Booty Green waved him silent and said, "Muthafucka, calm down! Don't talk about it, be about it! If you that muthafuckin' nervous, then take yo' high-yellow ass over there and kill that bitch and that lil' punk ass nigga!" The contempt was dripping from Booty Green's every word.

"You crying like a lil' bitch, mane. You worried about a goddamn youngsta, nigga. That little muthafucka ain't even old enough to know what's going on, playa," Rabbit reasoned.

"Mane, you niggas are talking to me like y'all done forgot who the fuck I am. I'm Yellow Shoes, nigga! I kills, that's what I do! I pimps, that's what I do! I'm just tryna tell you country ass niggas that dead men can't talk, and I ain't gonna tell on my muthafuckin' self!" He had begun to sweat "You know what, mane? Don't even worry about it, playas. I will take care of it!" he said.

******

Yellow Shoes pulled up in an empty lot across the street from Pearl and Charlie's house on Pine Street. He got on his car phone and placed a call to Pearl, careful to cover the phone to mask his voice. He explained that her husband and brother-in-law were dead, and that her best friend was dead. Then he abruptly hung up. He thought to himself, *Let the games begin!* He knew all too well that Pearl would panic and that the call would draw her out. He would let Pearl get outside of the Dallas city limits and then he would make his move.

******

As Pearl drove, she was thinking of all of the good times in her life. She passed by the R.C. Lounge, and she giggled at the thought of her husband, and just as quickly she began to cry at the finality of death.

She felt dead inside. She felt tired and worn out. She needed coffee.

Pearl pulled into the parking lot of Big World Grocery Store. They had good coffee, plus they stayed open 24/7 so they were always open. She went inside and saw a few of her friends, but they were acting funny, like they knew something that they weren't telling her. *Fuck them!* Pearl thought as she got her coffee and left.

She was passing by Henderson Chicken Shack and heading up Oakland Boulevard when it hit her. She knew exactly where she and Ju-Ju could go to be safe. Once she was safely away from the city, she would get a hotel room to gather her thoughts and get some rest.

Pearl made it to I-20 East, and drove until she decided to pull over in Longview Texas to get a hotel room and get some rest. She saw a sign for The Red Door Motel in the distance. It was perfect, right off of the freeway but still secluded. Plus, it was still dark outside so she was sure she could still manage to get some sleep.

As she pulled up in the front of the small motel to go inside and pay for a room, she didn't notice the black Lincoln pull up and park between two semi-trucks. She got her room keys, went back to her car and drove around to the back of the hotel where her room was located, and parked her Cadillac.

Yellow Shoes moved with cat-like swiftness, and before Pearl could get out of her car he had already made it to her car, put the gun in the window and whispered to her, "Bye-bye, bitch!" And just as she looked up, he pulled the trigger.

The shot was so loud that Julius Jr. jumped up with his thumb still in his mouth and sleep still in his eyes.

Just as Yellow Shoes was about to pull the trigger on Julius Jr., a big muscular white man that resembled a lumberjack yelled out from one of the semi-trucks, "Hey! What are you doing?"

Yellow Shoes ran towards the man with his gun pointed at him, and once he saw the gun he ducked his head back into the cab of his 18-wheeler.

Julius Jr. began to scream uncontrollably, because he could see his Aunt Pearl's brains splattered against the window and lying in her lap, and her head had a big hole in the temple. He couldn't see the man that shot her. He tried to get a good look at him but he was running too fast. Julius just wanted to go home. He wanted to be with his father; he wanted to be with his mother and his brothers and sisters.

But he was alone… all alone. It was way too quiet, and all he could hear was his Uncle Charlie's voice in his head telling him: *"When you look in the mirror, youngsta, when you are all alone, the person looking back at you in the mirror is the only person you can count on."*

And then Julius slept.

Chapter 18

My Father's Son

Julius sat in his 5x8 cell looking at pictures that his mother had sent to him; pictures of family parties, his brothers and sisters, and some of her new man.

Julius had been in TYC (Texas Youth Commission) for almost a year for getting caught at school with a 9mm pistol and a backpack full of $10 bags of weed. He had missed a majority of the school year, and turned fourteen years old inside of juvenile jail. He had been able to stay on track with his schoolwork so he hadn't been held back. If they let him go like his mother said they were, then he would be out in time to start 9th grade.

Julius had stayed out of trouble just long enough to make a good impression with the adult counselors, but he had caused just enough turmoil to maintain his reputation in "juvie". He smiled to himself because the adults really believed that incarceration was rehabilitation. In truth, he had learned how to be a better criminal.

Julius had started out moving a little weed every now and then, but the older cats in juvie had been talking about slinging crack. They said it looked like chipped off pieces of a tooth. They also said that it was less bulky than weed and it didn't leave an odor.

Julius had also become really good friends with a sixteen year old Mexican kid named Sleepy. He was always talking shit about how his uncles had all the raw powder in Dallas, and how the raw powder could be cooked to make crack cocaine.

Julius met the twins, Slow and Teddy. All they talked about were guns. They were from the Park Row section of South Dallas.

He'd also gotten interested in mathematics in juvenile because Number One: his math teacher was a sexy ass female; and Number 2: she equated everything to money, and Julius loved money.

His daydream was interrupted by the sound of the chow bell. It was time for lunch and he couldn't wait to get to the chow hall to see his homies. Chow time was always interesting to him because there was always something new to learn. The way he figured it, if he could use half of what he learned in kiddie prison, he would be rich by graduation.

He spotted Teddy across the chow hall. "Hey, what it is, cuzz?" Julius yelled across the cafeteria.

Teddy threw up a gang sign and went back to eating his lunch.

Julius got his lunch and joined the rest of the BG's (baby gangstas) and YG's (young gangstas) at the table where Teddy was sitting.

"Yeah, mane, these muthafuckas moved me to B-Block with all them muhfuckin' slobs, cuzz!" Slow exclaimed.

"Slob" was a term that the Crips used to disrespect and describe the Bloods. They also had other offensive names for the Bloods: "hulobs", "blobs" or "floods". These words generally pissed the young Bloods off. But the Bloods had derogatory names for the Crips as well. They would call them "crickets", "crabs", "erickets", "coons" and "cowards".

Teddy looked angry. He and Slow had never been apart, and he felt like the guards had separated them out of spite. "Man, them bitch ass CO's did that shit on purpose! It's almost like they wanna see a nigga scrappin' with them slobs!" Teddy said, obviously heated.

Bebo chimed in, "Cuzz you two niggas got a couple more weeks and y'all goin' home, so just chill and lay low, my nigga."

Bebo was a big kid from Dixon Circle. He and Julius knew each other from the neighborhood. All Bebo was into was stealing cars, and he was good at it.

"Yeah, I understand all that, but if something happens to my muthafuckin' brother, who's gonna explain that shit to my granny?" Teddy screamed.

"Man, ain't shit gonna happen to me, cuzz. Them slobs can't see me!" Slow said with a chuckle.

Slow and Teddy were equally dangerous, but for Teddy's angry and volatile nature, Slow was just the opposite. He was somewhat mellow and lighthearted.

"Ju, what you gonna do when you get out in three week, mane?" one of the BG's asked.

"Shit, first I'ma smoke me a fat ass joint, drink some Cisco, and then I'ma go find Jelly!"

They all laughed because they all knew better. Even though Jelly would sneak and write Julius every week, they all knew that Mrs. Gray would never let him near Jelly.

They all left the chow hall feeling good and laughing. As they passed a group of young Bloods they exchanged glances, but nobody disrespected or "set tripped" as they called it.

When Julius got back to his cell he thought to himself that he was coming into his own. He had in his time in juvenile been able to build himself a tight team of gangsters that were really loyal.

He smuggled money out through visitations, and his god brother, Ray always put part of the money away. Part of the money went to continue their criminal enterprise inside of the juvenile. Cigarettes were considered contraband in TYC, so if you could corrupt a CO then you could make good money.

Mrs. Cane was that CO. She had low self-esteem, didn't have any children, and wanted them desperately. She wanted to be down so badly that it was borderline pathetic, so when Julius went to her with the possibility of bringing in cigarettes, liquor and weed, of course she was hesitant, but he put on his best boyish charm and assured her that there was minimal risk.

A can of Top Menthol with 300 rolling papers sold for $2.50 in the store, but in juvenile, once you rolled all of the cigarettes and they sold for 50¢ apiece the profits were ridiculous.

Likewise, a fifth of E&J sold for $15, and they sold shots for $3 apiece. Julius would make sure that Mrs. Cane got $20 a can for the cigarettes and $40 for the fifth, and she would be happy. But once the demand got greater, she began to get nervous. That really didn't matter to Julius, because on the profit side after everybody had gotten paid, he had been able to save about $10,000 in profits.

Julius had already talked to Sleepy, and got a good price for a half a kilo. Sleepy had promised him that he could get his uncles to give it to him for $8,000, and that it would be 95% pure. He also had promised that since Julius would be his customer, he would show him how to cut and cook the cocaine to make crack to maximize his profits. Now with less than a month to go, all he had to do was keep his nose clean and it was on when he got out.

Julius lay back on his bunk with his hand folded behind his head and began to daydream about Angelica, his sweet Jelly. She was what really kept him going. Sometimes it made him sad to think of her, because for some reason, just like today, his mind always shifted from Jelly to his father, Uncle Charlie and Auntie Pearl

Ever since their deaths, his mother had tiptoed around the truth with him, but he had heard rumors about what really happened. It always pissed him off because the words "murder", "betrayal" and fucked up things like that popped up. But his mother was only going by what she had heard in the streets.

The night that she was killed, his Aunt Pearl had called Najé and told her what had happened to Julius and Charlie, and that she had to to go into hiding to protect herself and Julius Jr.

When Julius had awakened the next morning, he was in a hospital bed and his mother was by his side.

Since she had gotten settled in Texas, his mother had found herself a job, found a man, and was living an impressive life. Her "man" had so much money that it was unreal, and it seemed as though before she could even ask for it she already had it. Jewelry? No problem. A fur coat? No problem. Designer clothes? No problem. Whatever she wanted, she got it.

Najé sent Julius money and pictures of his family, and her man seemed pretty cool. Julius hadn't gotten a chance to know him yet, but he seemed okay. He just couldn't wait to go home.

His mother had told him that they had moved and sent pictures of the new house. Julius had his own room, a stereo, a TV, a moped, and basically whatever he wanted. He was happy that his mother was happy and not stressing.

"Man, what the fuck you thinkin' about?" Casper asked, breaking Julius out of his daydream.

Casper was a fat albino kid that Julius met inside. He had an easy smile and bright eyes. To meet him you would automatically think that he was too friendly, but that was just Casper. They called him "Casper" because he was as white as a ghost.

Julius managed a weak smile and a nod. "What up, homey?"

"Not shit. Just about to hit the yard. You coming?"

"Yeah, I'll be out in a minute." Julius watched Casper walk away, wondering how the young man could smile knowing he was never going home.

Casper smiled a lot, but he was a killer. He was fifteen years old and had been locked up in TYC since he was twelve, convicted of killing his entire family; his mother, his father and his two older sisters. He told Julius that he had killed his parents because he didn't feel like they loved him, and he killed his sisters because they always teased him by telling him that God didn't love him, and that he was a retard because he was albino.

Julius personally thought that the nigga was crazy, because the whole time he was telling Julius about the murders he was smiling. He had told Julius how he had slit his father's throat, and when his mother heard his father gurgling blood she woke up, and he had stabbed her in her eye before she could scream. He had raped both of his sisters after he had cut their throats, and then just called the police and waited for them to pick him up. All the while he was smiling, and it gave Julius the shivers.

As Julius slid on his Nikes and headed towards the rec yard, he felt that funny feeling in the pit of his stomach that he always got when something was going to happen, but he dismissed it and walked out onto the rec yard just in time for mail call.

It was always the same ritual. The cats who knew they had mail were over-anxious and were always up front. The dude's that were hopeful but not quite sure whether they had mail or not were in the middle, and the ones that knew they had mail but were too cool to look anxious played the back. The guys that knew they never got mail just wandered the yard aimlessly during mail call, some talking, some working out, some playing basketball, and others just random horse playing.

It was easy for Julius to get caught up and forget that he was a kid himself. His mind was always somewhere else, and his father had told him that he had an old soul.

The fat black guard called his name. Julius' mother had written him a letter, and he thought to himself, *Here we go again! More pictures to make me home sick.* He walked to a big shade tree out by the portables and away from the noise, and sat on a picnic table and read the letter:

My dearest Chocolate Chip:

Hello, son of mine! By the time this letter reaches you I hope it finds you in the very best of God's gracious care. As for me, I'm fine.

I'm writing this letter to let you know that I am looking forward to your release. I'm anxious for you to come and stay with Irvin and me. I sent you pictures of your room, but the pictures don't do it any justice. I miss you, honey.

Your education is what's most important to me. Hopefully you have been thinking about what school you want to go to when you come home. You are your father's son, and his blood runs through your veins. You're a natural hustler and a natural born gangster but, you're also half my blood, and my half is artistic, educated and curious. Use what God has given you, sweetie, or He just may take it away.

I'm afraid for you sometimes, baby; afraid because you're a 14 year old kid with a 40 year old mind; afraid for you because you hold in your emotions and you don't share how you feel! You have yet to show any emotion concerning your father, your uncle, and your aunt, and that scares me.

Well, I don't want to talk your head off, honey, sooooo... until those gates clang loudly behind you,

Love Always,
Your Mommy, Najé

P.S. None of your sisters or brothers know that you are in jail. I prefer to keep it that way because it's not their business.

Julius just smiled. He knew his mother well enough to know two things: One: her letter was a way to make amends on a strained relationship; and Two: her P.S. was exactly what it implied; it was none of their damned business. The way his mother saw it, their relationship might be strained, but he was still her youngest, her baby boy of six kids, so she had a special place in her heart for him. In her eyes, he was special and he deserved every affordable opportunity to get his life on the right track.

The count time bell sounded and Julius made his way to his dorm, hoping that his last three weeks in this hell hole would pass quickly. He had a lot of planning to do within the next three weeks, and he also had a lot of decisions to make. He knew things wouldn't be easy but he was prepared for the challenge.

Sleepy came into Julius' cell with a smirk on his face, and he looked the young Mexican up and down. Two weeks had passed by quickly, and Sleepy was going home. He was going to be Julius' main connect when he got out, so they had gotten pretty tight.

"S'up, *vato*? I'm going home tomorrow, homes," Sleepy said while trying not to let his excitement show.

"Yeah, I know, cuzz. Shit, you act like you ain't excited and shit," Julius teased.

"I am excited, homey. It's just all business once I hit the streets. My uncles are having me home schooled because they don't want me distracted. But maybe when you come home they'll let me go to public school if shit goes right." Sleepy had a faraway look in his eyes when he said that.

Julius began speaking slowly, mainly so that he was sure that Sleepy got a clear understanding of where he was coming from. "Listen, bro. We're gonna do business, and we're gonna be family like we talked about. But I will have to maintain my grades and fly underneath the radar to keep my mother off my ass. So if your uncles do let you go to public school, don't think I'm acting funny if I'm 'bout my books during school, know what I'm saying, homey?" Julius smirked.

The two young men shook hands. No words needed to be spoken because Sleepy knew that Julius was about his business. He also knew that there was coldness to this *miate,* and he would have to be watched.

******

The day before Julius was supposed to leave he called a meeting on the rec yard. Most of the cats that he considered himself really close to had gone home already.

Slow was still there on "closed custody" because he had been fighting with the Bloods, and had three more months to do. Sleepy was gone, Teddy was gone and Bebo was gone too. Casper was there, but he wasn't going home. The closest he would ever get to going home was to be transferred to TDC (Texas Department of Corrections) on his eighteenth birthday. Julius had foot soldiers there that had either not proven themselves yet, or who he didn't feel were smart enough to move up in rank too quickly.

It was noisy because they were excited. The big homey, Julius never called a meeting unless it was good news. He didn't believe in calling them together for bad news unless it was absolutely necessary.

"Quiet down! Quiet down, and listen up, because I don't wanna hafta talk loud over you niggas, and I'm only gonna say this shit once! As all of you know, I'm going home tomorrow. My YG's, Slow and Casper are gonna run the cigarettes, liquor and weed. The more work you BG's put in, the quicker you can move up in rank. Best believe I'ma hear about who's doing what out on the streets, so when you come home if you ain't been putting in work, the OG's out on the block are gonna know about it, you can trust that! The same pay scale applies, so if you're getting down you shouldn't need to worry your folks for no bread. It won't be a bunch of letters and shit written, so don't expect none. I will write either Slow or Casper every other week and let them know the deal. Any questions?"

"Yeah, big homey, I got one," came a voice from the back of the crowd. It was an eleven year old youngster named Shy who was shy and withdrawn, but he was a stone cold hustler. He was so little that he could get into places that most youngsters couldn't get into. Julius really liked him because even though he was little, he was down for the set. No matter what Julius asked him to do, he did it. He loved being a Crip that much.

"Shy, what up, cuzz?" Julius asked.

"Yeah, cuzz, I'm coming home in two months and my momma says I can't come to her house. I don't have nowhere to go so my counselor says they're prob'ly gonna put me in foster care, cuzz!" Shy said.

Julius knew that Shy would probably end up at Buckner Youth Home in Pleasant Grove. It was a cross between juvenile and foster care, but strictly for throwaways. "Naw, cuzz. Maybe my T-Jones will let you come to the crib and stay with us. Just hold tight, lil' homey," Julius said flatly. "Any more questions?" he asked. There were none.

With that, he jumped down off the picnic table and headed for his cell to pack his things. Tonight was going to be a long night.

Slow had followed him back to his cell, and Julius handed him a shoebox filled with weed and cigarettes, and a commissary bag filled with bottles of liquor. There was no need to count or talk about the money. Slow was Julius' right-hand man, and Julius trusted him.

"Damn, cuzz, I'ma miss you, my nigga. Who's gonna keep these knuckleheads in line when you're gone?" Slow asked, half joking.

"I ain't worried about that, cuzz. Shiiiiit, I already know you can handle this shit!"

They laughed and shared a G hug, where they would hug one another and draw giant C's on one another's backs with their left hands.

After Slow left, Casper stopped by. He stood in Julius' doorway for a long time just looking at him with tears in his eyes. Julius was getting a little freaked out but he just waited, and finally Casper began to speak.

"Say, mane, I just wanna say thank you, cuzz. First off, thank you, because I ain't never ran shit. And second of all, thank you for accepting me for who I am, homey." He smiled and walked away.

Julius got visits for the next hour and a half, and by the time the guys finished coming by he was dog ass tired. He lay back on his bunk and dozed off, hoping that tomorrow when he got out he would see Jelly.

It seemed like he had only been asleep for a few seconds before a flashlight in his eyes woke him up.

"Gage, roll it up! Hat on tight! You're going home!"

Chapter 19

Mama's Chocolate Chip

Najé Dunn loved all of her children equally, but her youngest—her chocolate chip—was special. He was the last "pea out of the pod", and he had some of the craziest notions and ideologies she'd ever heard of, but they all made sense.

The older he got, the more like his father he began to look and act; to the point it was almost scary. Najé thought it was spooky. He could be eerily calm, but you could always see the fire in his eyes. You could always tell that if necessary, he would go off, and that in itself scared her because she didn't want to lose her baby boy to the streets like she had lost his father.

Julius had in his mind that Najé didn't love him because she had let his father take him when they'd split up. She had cried many nights about her decision, but she was a woman of her word. She had given Big Julius her word that if they ever divorced that he could raise his youngest son. She had agreed to this out of love and admiration for Julius Sr. Knowing what she knew about him and his family, he was by definition a hell of a man. And now she had to make her baby boy understand the pact that his parents had made. She loved her youngest son enough to die for him if necessary, but she had a feeling that it would not be necessary. Julius was more than capable of taking care of himself.

At fourteen years old, Julius was more mature than a lot of people twice... three times his age. The only thing Najé worried a little bit about was how he and her man, Irving would get along. Irving was a hustler and he ran the streets, but he never brought it home with him. Julius had met him, but since he had been in juvie things had gotten a little more serious and they had moved in together.

Irving always seemed to keep Najé insulated from the street life. Of course she knew what he did, and she heard stories in the streets, but he treated her like a queen. They stayed in South Dallas, but they had a really nice house in the upper class section of the south side. They had a house in the Forest Avenue section which was considered upper class because it used to be owned and inhabited by Jews, and most of them were very affluent so the houses resembled mini-mansions and were very expensive.

Najé's home had six bedrooms and three bathrooms, and a huge back yard with a swimming pool. Her friends were all influential people in the black community. In the house to the left of hers the news anchor, Clarice Tinsley lived, and on the right was where City Councilman John Wiley Price lived.

Najé was careful to not be seen as "bougie" by friends or family. She was always down to earth and always tried to help when she could.

Now all she wanted was for her baby boy to come home and do what he was supposed to do. Everything and everybody was ready for his homecoming. The world was his to conquer.

But her maternal instincts had her worried about her son.

Chapter 20

Dude Seems Okay

Julius considered himself extremely lucky and blessed. He had come home at fourteen years old basically a grown man. His mother and Irving had gotten married, and he had to admit that the dude was cool. Anything he or his mother asked for was freely given.

Julius was sixteen years old now, and he still had the same friends and was still making money hand over fist on the low. The money was coming in so regularly that Julius knew his mother had to know what he was doing because she would make little remarks here and there.

Once when he had gotten all A's on his report card his mother was about to give him a $100 bill, but she stopped suddenly and remarked, "You should be giving *me* a $100, 'Mr. High Roller!'" It shocked him at first, but he dismissed it just as quickly.

His mother always made little slick ass comments like that, so it was nothing new. Besides, if she put him out for hustling, his girlfriend, Shuntae was twenty three years old, and she wanted him to move in with her anyway.

But Julius wasn't dumb. He knew that Shuntae was only after the money. She was twenty three and he was sixteen, and the only thing they had in common was sex. Julius was inexperienced at sex and she knew that and used it to her advantage. She did and said things to him sexually that would've driven the average young boy crazy. But Julius took it all in stride.

His aces in the game used to stay on his shit about her. Ray used to make statements like, "Nigga, money yo' bitch!" or "Nigga, you married to the game!" or "Money over bitches, fool! Fuck a bitch!"

And Shy never let him forget his priorities. He always reminded Julius that his focus should be on school and money, that's all. Julius understood this, and he loved nothing more than money... well, he loved Angelica too. But she had made it clear that they couldn't be together. She wanted to change him and wanted him to leave the streets and be a square to impress her mother. Julius wasn't trying to hear that so he kept his distance.

Shy had been staying with Julius and his family since his release, and they had become even better friends. Julius still hung out with his old crowd, but Shy was different. He was young, but his mentality was so on point that it amazed Julius. He wasn't flashy, he wasn't loud, he was actually low key and Julius liked that. Shy could make $5,000 in one week and nobody would ever know it.

Julius was lying in bed thinking when Shy walked in. "What it was, cuzz?" Shy asked.

"Shit, just chillin', lil' homie. You get them ends from Bean?" Julius asked.

"Yeah, I met him down at the pool hall on Pine and Colonial, but I had to wait because your step-pops was in that bitch!" Shy didn't like Irving, and every chance he got he would tell Julius that something wasn't right about him.

"Mane, Irv's a cool muthafucka and he makes my momma happy. That's all that matters to me, cuzz!" Julius barked.

Shy let it go. He knew when his friend was irritated. "If you need me I'll be in my room," Shy said.

Julius had more on his mind than a petty beef. On his mind was money, and lots of it. He had come up with a plan to get it. These petty crack sales weren't bringing in the profits that he wanted to make. His gang was getting more and more powerful every day, but he felt like he was standing still.

Dixon Circle 357um practically owned South Dallas. Sure there were other Crip sets in the south side, but Dixon Circle was the most powerful and the most feared by far. Everybody had a hand in making the neighborhood work like a well-tuned machine. In Dixon, either you were a killer, a schoolboy, or a drug dealer, and Julius was all three and he wanted to be respected as such. He had a plan, but in order to pull it off he would need all of his boys on the same page.

The plan was simple: the Jamaican Posse was moving into Dallas and spreading fast. Ever since Julius had been watching them, he discovered that they operated out of a central location at a little bar called the Silver Slipper. The Jamaicans came in Posses, and each Posse would have a captain, and that captain would always hire young junior high and high school students, because they knew that if they got busted they would only get a slap on the wrist.

Julius had been watching closely at their routine, and his plan was to rob the Jamaicans not just once, but every chance he got. He had counted forty crack houses owned by them. He reasoned that if he and his boys robbed them they couldn't call the police. Therefore, they would be free to take the money and drugs and help their neighborhood. Who could the Jamaicans tell? They were doing wrong themselves.

Julius got on the phone and called everyone that he thought might be down for getting that money, but he only called people that he knew he could count on and trust. "Shy, round up all the little homeys and have them meet us in the graveyard behind Lincoln High."

Julius only had six dudes that he trusted beyond a shadow of a doubt, and those six had guys under them that were extremely loyal to them.

Shy was first. He was like a brother to Julius.

And then there was Ray. He was a real go-getter and was always about his hustle. Ray's father didn't like him much, and always said that he should've just worn a rubber instead of getting Ray's mother pregnant because Ray was a bad seed. That only made Ray hustle even harder and stay in the streets more. His father was a real cutthroat dude, but only when he was drinking. When he was sober he was "Cliff Huxtable" in the flesh.

Duddy and D-Train were OG's to Julius, but if there was a lick to be hit they wanted in on it for certain, and they would gladly play their roles to get it. Duddy and D-Train were twins, but they were so different that a lot of people didn't even believe that they were brothers, let alone twins. Duddy was light skinned and stocky with a low haircut and kind of a pretty boy, but he was a gangster to the heart. D-

119

Train, on the other hand, was as black as midnight, tall with a skinny frame, and had long corn rowed braids. You could set the clock by those two brothers, which in Julius' mind wasn't necessarily a good thing because they had the same routine every day: Wake up, cop some weed from Collins Street, grab some papers and a 40oz. of Old English from the "second store" and hit the block. Day in and day out it was the same old shit.

Then you had cockeyed Kenneth. This cat was down with just about anything Julius said or did. His father was in prison and his mother was holding down two jobs trying to take care of him and his two brothers. So whatever he could do to bring something to the table he was with it.

Last but not least he contacted his Mexican partner from juvie, Sleepy. He and Sleepy talked a long time about what the plan was, and Julius was comfortable and confident about bringing the young Mexican in on the deal. Sleepy's uncles had agreed to supply the young hoodlums with all of the firepower they would need, for a small fee. They didn't want money, they wanted assurances; assurance that the Rastas wouldn't be a problem anymore. This would be a win-win situation for the Mexicans. The Jamaicans had been a thorn in their asses since they came to Dallas, so if it cost them a few guns to get the Rasta's out of their mix, then that was a price that they would gladly pay.

******

It was dark outside and the moon cast an eerie glow across the young gangsters in the graveyard as Julius began to speak. "Listen up, my niggas. Some of y'all know why you're here, and for those that don't know, I'ma make it real clear: money, bread, cheese, scrilla… all of the above!"

He paused to let his words sink in. He looked over the crowd of young gangsters, and in addition to his six guys, he saw twenty more BG's and YG's there to put in work. By his calculation that added up to seven squads, with four gangsters to a squad.

He continued. "Dawg, it don't take no rocket scientist to see what's going on in the South Side, mane. The Jamaicans are moving up in this bitch, taking over all the dope holes, from Grand Ave. clean over to Bon Ton. Those muthafuckas are opening up shop and killing anybody that they feel is in the way. Nigga's are getting smoked every day because those muthafuckas is heartless, cuzz!"

Julius had to pause to calm himself down. He always got overly excited when the subject of territory came up. "If you're about your muthafuckin' paper, then this should be right up your alley. We gonna hit these muthafuckas every day until they close up shop. It don't matter where these dreadlock wearing bitches are doing business; we're closing their shit up! If you ain't with it just say the word. No harm no foul, but speak now or forever hold your goddamn peace!" he screamed.

A loud cheer went across the graveyard, signaling that everybody in attendance was with it.

"These niggas right here are gonna pick their squads: Duddy, D-Train, Kenneth, Shy and Sleepy, come up here, mane. If this shit goes down the way we plan for it to, we're gonna have enough money and dope to run Dallas!"

Each man picked a crew of three men. With them now in squads, Julius brought his voice down almost to a whisper. "Lookout, playas! We gonna hit seven spots simultaneously every day until these bitch ass niggas leave South Dallas." He grinned. "Sleepy's uncles, in addition to supplying the guns, are supplying seven unmarked white cargo vans to pull off the 'kick in the door' burglaries. We 'bout to be paid, niggas!" Julius exclaimed. With that being said, he handed each one of his head men a different address. "Set your watches to 1:30 a.m. At exactly 1:30 a.m. we strike! They won't know what hit that ass!"

Chapter 21

Karma's a Real Bitch

Julius sat in the parking lot in his white panel van, silently thinking. Every now and then he would glance down at his watch. It was 12:50 a.m., 40 more minutes and it was going down. His heart was pounding, not from fear but from excitement. When these heists went down it would make his clique wealthy enough to not need the Mexicans. They could buy their kilos directly from the Columbians and cut out the middleman if he could get the connection.

Julius looked down at his watch again and saw that it was 1:00 a.m. *Damn, time is creeping!* he thought.

Just then, a Dallas police car cruised by slowly and Julius tensed up, but dismissed it just as quickly because those "creep by" moves were routine around this time of morning.

When 1:30 came it was pitch black and silent outside. They moved quickly and quietly to their predetermined destination.

BlaccTopp

Julius knocked on the apartment door while his team was waiting off to the sides. He knocked once more, and from behind the door he heard a groggy, gravelly voice with a thick heavy West Indian accent ask, "Yeah, mon?"

Julius said in mock excitement, "I need something, dawg! I need an onion!"

The sleepy Jamaican opened the door and never knew what hit him. Julius' team rushed through the door with their guns drawn. Julius leered at the Jamaican and said, "Listen here, you curried goat eating muthafucka! I don't wanna hurt you, but I will if you get to bullshittin'! Now where it's at?"

He got no response.

"Where's the money and shit?"

Again no response.

Julius cocked his pistol and slapped the man across the face, and then shoved his gun into the man's mouth and brought his voice down to a deadly whisper. "Listen, muthafucka! You can either tell me where the shit is, or I can kill you and search for it myself! It's your goddamn choice!"

The older man began to whimper, softly at first then loud uncontrollable sobs.

Julius slapped him again. "Where, nigga?" he demanded.

The old Jamaican composed himself enough to speak. "Youth, what you gwan do wit' me fo' me tell you what you wan know? You gwan dead me?" he said, obviously shaken.

"Naw, old man, I ain't gonna touch you!" Julius said with a smirk.

124

The old man let out a sigh of relief and managed a weak smile. "De money is in de attic, and dem drugs, dem is in de room in a trunk by de bed, mon."

Julius sent one kid for the money, another for the drugs, and the last kid he kept with him; a dark skinned kid with pop eyes, a low haircut and bulging muscles who everyone called Spooky.

The first kid came back with a big green army duffel bag full of money and a big ass smile on his face. The second kid came out of the bedroom dragging a footlocker. He nodded to Julius, and Julius in turn nodded to Spooky, who grabbed the old man's head, yanked it back and slit his throat.

It seemed like it had taken a very long time, but in reality it had only taken 15 minutes. They were in and out by 1:45a.m.

All across the city Julius' gang had carried out the same brutal plans. One by one the white panel vans began to roll into an empty warehouse on Gaston Ave., which Sleepy's uncles owned.

Julius decided that they would use this warehouse for a base of operations, partly because it was large enough to hold all of the cargo vans, and partly because with Sleepy's uncles being the owners, him and his gang could come and go as they pleased. It was close enough to his house to get there in a hurry if necessary.

Once inside the warehouse, Julius gave a quick headcount to make sure that everybody was there. He didn't want anybody to get hurt, but he also didn't want niggas getting sticky fingers and running off with the money that they had robbed. He was all about the "honor among thieves" rule.

"Okay, so everybody is accounted for. I need all of the squad leaders to bring what they got out of the Dreads to the table," he said, knowing that the take from the robberies would be substantial. He knew this because all of the trap houses that they had hit were weight houses. He concentrated their efforts on the weight houses because the nickel and dime houses had to go to the weight houses to drop off money and pick up more dope anyway. If they could run the weight houses out of business, then the smaller nickel and dime houses – the twenty and fifty slab houses – would be on standby with the re-up money, giving them the perfect opportunity to hit them too. But he also knew that would cause the Jamaicans to beef up security. There would be more money, but there would also be greater risk to his guys.

All of his squad leaders had circled the table where Julius sat. They sat and they counted the money, and it seemed as though they had been counting for hours. They had gotten fifteen kilos and nine ounces of powder cocaine, and another four kilos of heroin. Plus, after all the money had been counted it came up to an astounding $160,000.

Julius just stared in disbelief, showing no emotion about one of his biggest takes during a robbery. He had begun to do quick mathematics in his head. The math had to be right, because he not only wanted his guys to be happy and satisfied, but he was also thinking about tomorrow.

He gave everybody in attendance $2,000 for their pockets, and a quarter of a kilo to work on the streets. He noticed a few guys looking at one another like they were being taken advantage of, and before it could become a problem Julius squashed it. "Dawg, I don't have any reason to fuck over nobody in this bitch!" he began. "If I divvy up this muthafuckin' money and dope evenly, niggas is gonna start high cappin' and getting flashy, and a whole lotta heat's gonna come down on us, and I'm sure nobody wants to go to jail or end up dead. And even though I don't need to explain myself, I will!" Now Julius had everyone's undivided attention.

"We're still young, mane, and we can't count on anybody but ourselves. The dope I gave y'all you earned; the money I gave y'all you earned. The dope and money that's left we're going to sell. We're gonna give the OG's in the 'hood some of the money, and give the Mexicans some for helping us out with the vans and shit. There's plenty more money coming, trust me, mane." Julius was finished talking, and if that wasn't good enough for an explanation, tough shit! Where else could you go and make $2,000 cash and $5,000 worth of dope in fifteen minutes? No fucking where!

Duddy and D-Train hadn't stayed behind after they dropped their van off. They had only dropped off the drugs, money and the van. Julius contacted Duddy and D-Train and told them he had something for them and something for the 'hood. He also contacted Sleepy's uncles and told them that it was urgent that he speak with them.

He waited until everybody was gone and pulled the vans in line one by one. Then he walked the entire warehouse making sure all of the windows and doors were locked.

After he was satisfied that the building was secure, he began to scout the warehouse to find the best place to hide the money and dope. He found an old Jobox toolbox that was bolted to the floor, and it had a big brass Master lock on it. He went into the office. He was sure there had to be keys in there somewhere. If he could get the lock off tonight, he could go and buy one later on that morning. He forced the top desk drawer open and found no keys; just a couple of *Playboy* magazines, a jar of Vaseline and a pack of Winston cigarettes. He checked the other drawers in the desk and found no keys.

Julius stood there frustrated. Looking around the office he noticed a box on the wall that had the word "Keys"on it and laughed at himself. "Dumb ass!" he said out loud. He opened the box to find that every key in the lock box was labeled, which would make his job a lot easier. There in plain sight was a key marked "Jobox". He took all of the keys and put them in his pockut, except for the Jobox key. He took out two kilos and $16,000 for the OG's, and took out $10,000 for the Mexicans. That left six kilos of cocaine and four kilos of heroin, and $80,000, all of which he put into the Jobox.

Julius needed more time to devise a plan to move the dope. There was no way he could take it home with him. His mother was too nosy. If she ever found it there would be problems; the kind of problems that a sixteen year old didn't want to face in dealing with his mother.

There was a loud knock on the big metal sliding doors, and Julius rushed up the stairs to the window overlooking the parking lot outside. Duddy's Cadillac and the Mexicans' Limousine were both outside. *Perfect timing!* he thought. He made his way to the door, pistol in hand, and opened it.

"What it was, cuzz?" D-Train said. That was the standard greeting among Crips. They embraced and gave each other G hugs. Julius did the same with Duddy.

When the Mexicans walked in the greeting was a little more jovial, but still along those lines. *"Odalé, chabalito!"* one of them said. The other Mexican just nodded to Julius.

"Okay, so I know y'all are probably wondering why I called y'all down here, right?" Julius said, showing obvious excitement.

The older Mexican finally spoke with a thick Spanish accent. "Yes, *vato*, I would like to know why I am out of my bed at the crack of dawn."

"Well, *jeffe*, I wanted to pay a tribute to the Cartel, and since y'all put us down with the vans and guns and the warehouse, I wanted to show my appreciation." With that being said, Julius handed the older Mexican a manila envelope containing the $10,000.

"There's more where that came from, *jeffe*. This is just the first of many. We are going to hit them hard until they run back to Jamaica!"

The older Mexican looked inside the envelope, then at Julius and gave a wicked smile, *"Chabalito*, I told you that money was not necessary and yet you still pay tribute. You are growing into an honorable young man, *vato*."

The two Mexicans turned and left. After seeing them to the door, Julius turned to his OG's and smiled. "Cuzz, we hit a major lick, my niggas! This is a tribute for the 'hood. It's $16,000 and two kilos. We got more licks to hit, just be ready. It's all about coming up."

The two OG's looked at each other. "Lil' homey, this work we put in was good work, huh? We gonna put this shit to work in the 'hood," Duddy said.

As Julius walked Duddy and D-Train to their car he asked, "Hey, cuzz do you niggas think y'all can drop me off at the Home Depot up the street?"

129

Duddy nodded. "No problem, cuzzin'."

Julius was wrapped up in his thoughts. He would have to find a way to move the dope without raising suspicions. He also had to take care of his business without raising his mother's suspicions, and most of all, he had to maintain his grades. Any slippage of his GPA would alarm her and his stepfather, and they would start to pry and get nosy. His stepfather would start running his mouth about things he'd heard on the streets, and he couldn't afford to take that chance. He liked his stepfather, but Julius had heard some things on the streets that didn't sit well with him. But then again, the streets were always talking, and you couldn't believe anything that you heard and only half what you saw. The streets had a way of holding court on its own, being both judge and jury. So if things weren't right with dude, they would work themselves out.

Julius ran into the Home Depot and got his lock. He was in and out quickly, and Duddy and D-Train dropped him back off at the warehouse.

Once he was satisfied that everything was locked up tight, he locked up the warehouse and walked across the street to the corner store to call a cab.

It was Saturday morning, and Julius always cut the grass on Saturday mornings. His stepfather would give him $25 or $30 for doing this chore. The money was cool when he was fourteen years old, but there really wasn't much he could do with $25 nowadays. Julius laughed about it. Pop's intentions were good, but if he had any idea how much money Julius was making and had the potential to make, he would be green with envy. But Julius mainly did it to keep his mother happy. He loved his mother. She was a good woman, and an all around good person. He knew that she had to have flaws, and if she did he didn't see them.

When Julius' cab finally arrived it finally dawned on him that Shy had left with one of the other homies. He hoped he didn't go home, because if he did his mother would start grilling him about why he was home and Julius was still out. Shy was smart enough to skate around the questions, but as smart as Shy thought he was, Najé was smarter.

******

Shy had caught a cab back to South Dallas and got out at Little World Grocery Store. They served breakfast at the small store, and he wanted to eat before he made it home so that he could sleep in.

He was walking out of Little World when he was forced into a black van by one of the Jamaican Posses.

The Jamaican in charge, the one who was called Christopher, hit him violently across the face with the grip of his pistol. "Where de fuck is me bumba-clot drugs, dem?" Christopher asked him.

Shy didn't say a word; he just looked at the older Jamaican man with disdain and contempt.

Christopher struck the kid with a forceful blow to the mouth. "Tell me what I want to know, or me swear before Jah that I will dead your ras-clad right here!" he spat.

Shy lunged at the man, connecting wildly to his jaw, only to be hit in the head with the butt of a Mossberg 12 gauge shotgun.

"You hafta give it to de youth, boss. The little pussy-hole got a lot of nerve to be so young, mon," the Jamaican flunky giggled.

The men drove the teen to a dead-end street behind Lincoln High School and parked the van.

"Youth, me gwan give you one last chance to tell me de truth, otherwise you gwan die right here right now!" Christopher screamed.

Shy just stared blankly at the man. He turned and spit a wad of blood into the face of the "Man, I don't know who you dreadlock wearing, curry goat eating muthafucka's think y'all dealing with! Shit, even if I tell you what you think I know, you ho's are gonna kill me anyway. So handle yo' bitch ass business," the young man said matter of factly.

"Me can say one t'ing about you, youth. You are loyal but, your loyalty is misplaced, my youth. The ras-clad batty boys that you protect will die anyway, and you my son, gwan die anyway."

Shy lunged at the man again. If he was going to die he would go out fighting.

The burly Jamaican man with the loud giggle grabbed Shy from behind, pulled him close, and with one swift motion slit his throat from ear to ear.

Christopher gave the driver a signal, and he started to drive. He turned down Hatcher headed towards Bexar Street. The men found a secluded part of the street going in the direction of the Rhodes Terrace Projects and simply opened the doors and rolled Shy's body out of the van onto the cold hard asphalt.

The early morning streetlights shone brightly on the young man's body. He had died to protect the only friend he had ever had.

******

When Julius got home he could smell coffee brewing. He could also smell breakfast cooking. He walked into the kitchen and saw his mother sitting at the kitchen table taking long drags from a Virginia Slim menthol cigarette. She looked distant and withdrawn.

"What's wrong ma?" Julius said

"Sit down, baby. I need to talk to you," Najé said somberly.

Julius was thinking to himself, *Oh Lord, here we go!* But his Mother launched right into it.

"They found Shy dead this morning, baby. They found his body off of Bexar Street in Bon Ton, the poor baby. It was brutal, Julius. They cut his tongue out of his mouth and slit his throat!" She was trembling now and Julius was dazed.

Shy had just left him at three something in the morning, and it was barely 8:30 a.m. He felt guilty. He felt like it wouldn't have happened if he would've kept Shy with him. His mother's voice interrupted his thoughts.

"They tried to call his sorry ass mammy, but her phone is off... again! Why someone would want to do that to a fourteen year old boy, I have no idea. Ju, you know I've always let you be your own man and I have only tried to push you and motivate you positively." She took a long drag from her cigarette to let the weight of her words sink in. "But if Shy's blood is on your hands, if you're directly or indirectly responsible for that baby losing his life, we are going to have a problem, do you hear me?"

Julius looked at his Mother. His heart was heavy and his mind was racing. "Yes, ma'am," was all he could manage.

"Julius?"

"Yeah, Ma?"

"Whatever you and Shy got yourselves into, Jesus can fix it. I love you very much. 'Look to the Heavens from where your blessings come plenty'," she quoted from the Bible as she was fixing his plate of eggs, biscuits, smothered potatoes, salmon croquet patties, and Julius' favorite, Brer Rabbit syrup. "Now eat up, baby. That grass isn't going to cut itself!"

And with that she kissed him on the forehead and walked out of the kitchen, fearing for her youngest son's safety more than ever.

Chapter 22

Bonez In Yo' Closet

Irving Green was in love with his wife. Najé meant the world to him. He hustled, he worked hard, and he put in extra work to make sure he could give her the finer things in life.

Her son Julius was sixteen years old, and he was genuinely a good kid. He got good grades in school, was well mannered, well liked and good looking. But there were a few things about him that made Irving uneasy. First off, his eyes were too intense for a kid sixteen years old. Sometimes when Julius looked at him it was almost as if all of his secrets had been laid bare. It was also spooky how much young Julius looked like his father. It bothered him to think about the old days; especially the old days that involved Julius Gage.

His wife was a beautiful woman, and the thought of losing her made him cringe. She trusted him and she loved him, so it was important for him to keep it that way. He had met her while she was mourning the loss of her family members. She was new to Texas and didn't know anybody, only her son. She had confided in him that her ex-husband, his brother and his brother's wife had all been murdered, and she was in Texas to take care of her son. She said she had five other children, but none of them stayed at home except for Julius. He was her youngest.

Najé had made it clear to Irving that she was not interested in a serious relationship, but that had just made him work that much harder to prove to her that he was the man she needed. In the beginning he played her little "friendship" game, but slowly he began to wear her down.

But her son was a different story. He didn't seem to trust anybody, and the harder he tried to get close to him the further Julius seemed to drift away from him. The money and the fancy gifts didn't mean a thing to the youngster. Irving was always trying to buy him things, but Julius would just glance at them and mutter "Thanks." Irving knew that Julius had respect for him, but he wanted him to look at him like a father figure. But a small part of Irving knew that this would never happen.

He also knew that the things that you thought were well hidden would eventually be exposed. In other words, what was done in the dark would always come to light; it wasn't a matter of *if* they would, it was a matter of *when*. And when the shit hits the fan there could be major problems ahead. He could only hope that when that time came it didn't drive a wedge between him and his Najé. He'd rather die than to live without her, and he'd rather kill her than let her go. His was a sick love, and he was fully aware of it.

Chapter 23

Relax Your Mind

Najé stood at the living room window watching her husband sitting in his truck and smoking a joint. Something was bothering him, because that was the only time that he smoked marijuana. He swore it calmed him down, but truth be told it just got him high and made him sleepy. But whatever made him happy made her happy. She didn't like pressing her husband about anything, but she really needed to know what was going on. This went beyond his strained relationship with her son. It was deeper than his company handing out layoffs, and she knew it wasn't her, because she did everything in her power to cater to him and keep him happy.

He was tossing and turning in his sleep like he was fighting in his dreams. He also muttered inaudible sentences that she couldn't make out except for a few words here… "Forgive me!" A few words there… "Love you!"… Always low and muffled.

She loved her husband, and whatever the problem was she would be in his corner rain or shine.

With death came a certain kind of enlightenment, not only within her, but also within Julius. Her baby boy had taken Shy's death hard. He didn't really show an abundance of emotion, but his actions were loud and clear. Julius had thrown himself into his activities full steam ahead.

Najé barely saw him during the day, but it was summer so she didn't really sweat it. Plus, this coming year would be his last year in school, so she was very excited about that. She was especially happy that he had been spending a lot of time with Angelica. Najé really liked her, and once Julius had gotten on point with his studies Angelica's mother had really warmed up to him. He was carrying a 3.6 GPA, and Najé was tickled pink about that.

Angelica was helping him study for his SAT's, and Julius had jokingly stated to Najé that he would be the first gangster in South Dallas history to get a perfect score on his SAT's. They'd had a good laugh about it, but truth of the matter was that she knew that her son was very capable of getting a perfect score—or very close to it—if he applied himself.

Najé pulled herself out of her reverie and walked to the front door to call for husband. "Irving, are you going to just sit out there in that car, stinking up the neighborhood smoking the devil's lettuce?" she said.

They both laughed as Irving got out of his car. He walked up onto the porch and greeted his wife with a warm, passionate kiss. "Hey there, beautiful! How goes it?" he said playfully as he cupped his wife's round, firm butt.

"Hey, Mr. Booty Green! I thought you had gotten lost and couldn't find your way home!" Najé joked.

"Shiiiiiit, I'd rather run through hell with gasoline draws on than to stay away from you, lil' girl!" Booty Green said. "Where's baby boy?" he asked as an afterthought.

"Child, you already know he's at Angelica's house. He spends more time there than he does at home. But she is good for him," Najé pointed out.

Irving "Booty" Green knew it was true. Julius and Angelica both wanted to go to college in Atlanta. Julius wanted to attend Morehouse and Angelica wanted to attend Spellman. These were both historically black universities, and that appealed to the teens.

Najé mused that Julius probably wanted to follow Angelica to Atlanta to get her away from her mother's watchful eye.

Julius had come home one day beyond excited and screamed, "She got in! She got into Spellman! She got a full scholarship, Ma!" He had picked his mother up and spun her around.

She loved to see her baby smile, and knew that when he got into Morehouse she would see that same big, bright smile.

Najé subconsciously did things to please Irving, especially on Friday's. Friday was the day that he got paid from his nine to five. Plus, he picked up all the money from the weed and bootleg houses that he owned in South Dallas. She used to feel like a gold digger until she remembered that she was his wife, and he had reminded her on numerous occasions that he loved giving her nice things. All she had to do was take care of him and stay fine! Shit, if she wanted to fix his favorite meal to make sure he was in a good mood and extra generous with the money, oh well! She had been in the kitchen all day cooking all of his favorites: smoked neck bones, collard greens, red beans and rice, and hot water cornbread. She had run his bath water when she heard him pull into the driveway, and she had rolled him two joints just the way he liked them. She knew her husband. She also knew that she would be Neiman Marcus bound on Saturday morning.

"Ooooo wee, baby! You got it smelling like Clara's Kitchen up in this thang, mama!" Green said, his mouth watering.

Clara's Kitchen was one of Booty Green's favorite restaurants, so Najé took that as a compliment. "Yeah, Daddy! Just the way you like it! You know I had to tickle your tummy, baby. You been working hard all day," she said in her sweetest and most innocent voice.

If she wasn't his wife he probably would've thought that she was trying to play him, but she deserved every penny he gave her. She worked every day and still came home and cooked and cleaned, so if she wanted to go shopping on the weekends he was happy to oblige.

Booty Green walked into his bedroom and saw that his pajamas had been laid out, along with his slippers and a couple of joints, and a little note that read:

> *Baby, I run your bath water, so go ahead and enjoy your nice hot bath and a joint and let me know when you're done so that I can dry you off and fix your plate.*
>
> *Love you,*
> *Najé*

He just smiled, thinking, *How did I get so lucky?*

Green grabbed a joint and slid into a tub of hot water. The thoughts going through his head were starting to get to him. The streets had begun to talk. His past was definitely catching up to him. The streets had begun to dredge up old memories of what happened to Chele, and what happened to Julius' father and the rest of his family. Some of the faint mutterings seemed to be on point, and some of them were laced with bullshit. Some of the other things he'd heard were so spectacular that he had to laugh to himself.

But this was no laughing matter. He was beginning to feel something that he didn't feel often... fear. Booty Green was afraid of three things:

First, he was afraid that when Najé found out the truth she would leave him.

Second, he was afraid that Julius Jr. would find out, and then he and his lil' gang banging ass friends would want to hold court in the streets.

And third, he was afraid to spend the rest of his life in prison. He wasn't considered an old dude, but he wasn't a youngster anymore either, so he would more than likely die in prison if he got a life sentence. He knew from a couple of his partners in prison doing life terms that he would have to pull at least 35 years before he would be eligible for parole.

Enough of that shit! Green thought. He wasn't planning on spending any amount of time in anybody's jailhouse. "Shit, I'm too big of a playa for anybody's muthafuckin' jail!" he said out loud.

Najé stood in the hallway silently watching her husband. He was a beautiful specimen of a man. Not too light skinned, but not as dark as Julius, he stood about 6' tall and weighed about 200 pounds, and was nicely built. He wasn't cut up and chiseled, but he still had an athletic body.

It was the kind of body reserved for men that worked in lumber yards. He had baby smooth skin and he never needed to shave.

Najé heard him say something about "jail" that abruptly ended her daydream. She would always stick by her man, but honestly, she had to think about Julius. What kind of potentially negative message could that send to her son? If she stayed by this man's side knowing he was guilty of whatever offense they would convict him for, how would Julius view that?

Then again, she could also be jumping the gun. It could be something simple like traffic tickets or something of that nature. Whatever it was, she would get the facts before she made any decisions.

Chapter 24

My Ballz and My Word

Julius was anxious and antsy. He wanted to know who had killed his best friend. It was eating at his soul like maggots on a corpse. He constantly felt sick to his stomach. He would eat, only to throw up whatever he had eaten.

Crying uncontrollably had become the norm for him, and he didn't like it. It made him feel weak and vulnerable, as if he had no control over his emotions. He felt like it was his fault that Shy was dead, and no matter how hard he tried he couldn't shake that feeling.

Julius had an army of soldiers on the streets and countless connections in the seedy underground of Dallas, so if the streets knew anything about the murder of his little homey, he would most certainly get to the bottom of it. With enough money circulating on the streets as a reward for any information, people would start singing like a church choir. He put the word out that any information about who had killed Shy was worth $10,000, and if the information was accurate another $15,000 would follow.

Within hours his pager had started to blow up with misinformation. For every call that he received, he would immediately dispatch one of his soldiers to check out the tip. Nothing seemed to pan out though, and Julius was getting frustrated, and was becoming furious. This wasn't a joking matter, and he had gotten the impression that instead of people beating the block trying to find out who killed his friend, they were willing to tell lies to make a quick buck.

Julius' pager began to vibrate again but, this number had a "911" trailer behind it, signifying an emergency or urgent signal, so the young gangster walked to the pay phone on the corner across the street from his house. When he dialed the number it rang continuously, and Julius had a sinking feeling in the pit of his stomach. *Could this be the real thing? Could this be the tip I've been waiting for?* Julius hung up the phone and redialed the number.

After a few short rings, a deep, scruffy voice answered. "Yo!" the voice said deeply from the other end of the phone.

Julius paused, unable to speak. This had to be a setup. But he decided that if it was a setup, then he would play along. "Yeah, what, up?"

"Listen, youth, and listen closely, mon. De Posse, dem killed your friend, you understand? And dem a get close to knowing who you be. If me was you, me would leave it be before Christopher and dem find out who you are, mon," the voice on the other end of the phone said flatly.

"And just who are you? And who the fuck is Christopher?" Julius asked.

"Mon, my name is unimportant. Just know dis. If me get your information this easy, just t'ink how easy

Christopher can get it. Dem a kill your youths to get to you!" the Jamaican said.

"And how do I know that this information is accurate and you're not trying to set me up?" Julius asked cautiously. "How are you going to pick up your reward money?"

The older Jamaican just laughed. "Me ain't want your money, youth. I want you to dead him. Dat bumba-clot mon, Christopher and his fuckery a make it hard fo' good shottas to get de ras-clad money. Keep your money, youth. Just get rid of that pussy-clad Christopher!" the Jamaican exclaimed.

Julius forcefully hung up the phone. He was furious. How dare these foreigners come to his country... his neighborhood and try and muscle his squad! He had to mobilize his boys and come up with a plan. He knew Duddy and D-Train would want to move quickly on the Jamaicans. But his father had always told him that piss poor planning leads to piss poor performance. Therefore, he had no plans on going into war with the Jamaicans half-cocked.

He paced up and down the sidewalk for a while just thinking. His next move had to be his best move. He had gangsters that relied on him to feed their families, and for a young man he took excellent care of the people underneath him.

He put in a call to Duddy.

"*Hello! You've reached Duddy. Leave me a message.* Bee-e-e-ep!"

Julius knew better than to leave a message on a machine but, he needed to talk to someone. He wished silently that his father was still alive. He wished that he had an older brother or a cousin; somebody that could tell him what to do. For the first time in a long time he was confused. He wasn't confused about going after the Jamaicans, that was a given. His retribution for the murder of Shy would be swift and exact.

He tried Duddy's number again, and this time he answered on the second ring. "What's up, little cuzz?" Duddy asked.

"I need to come and see you, cuzzo. We have a problem," Julius explained.

"Shit, I just walk in the crib nigga. Come through."

Julius hung up the phone and called a cab. It seemed to take an eternity for the cab to come, and during that time he had come up with what he believed was a viable plan to get back at the Jamaicans. But it would have to be perfect timing.

The taxi arrived, and Julius cautiously looked inside with his hand underneath his shirt, ready for anything that might happen. "Ay, take me down to Dixon, bruh. Prince Hall Apartments," Julius ordered.

Once down on Dixon, the young hustler paid the cabby and walked to the back of the apartment complex. Duddy and D-Train had a cook house in the back where a lot of the young gangsters would hang out from time to time.

Julius walked through the complex with his eyes darting from side to side and up and down. He felt paranoid, but with money floating around it was hard to know exactly who could be trusted.

He stepped around a corner and saw one of his homies, Moon leaning against a brick wall with a female crack head kneeling between his legs, giving him head.

"What up, little gangsta?" Moon said with a knowing smirk on his face.

Julius dropped his head, threw up two fingers and kept walking. *Niggas will get their dick sucked anywhere,* he thought. He silently chuckled to himself and increased his speed towards Duddy's cook house.

He reached the cook house door where Duddy and his twin brother cooked up their drugs. They had replaced the wooden door with a heavy reinforced steel one. It was heavy, and it made Julius' knuckles hurt every time he knocked on it. He hated that door, but it was a necessary evil to protect the business that they had going on inside of the apartment.

Julius took out his pistol and knocked on the door with it. Three quick taps, five slow taps and then seven quick taps was the signal. The gang members inside the trap house knew what to listen for. That was the signal for 357um members. Fiends were never allowed inside because the house was a cook house, and fiends didn't buy weight.

Julius stepped inside and immediately headed to the back of the apartment where Duddy was waiting with D-Train. He didn't waste any time launching into the situation. "Cuzz, the Jamaicans killed Shy! I haven't learned all of the details yet, but I know the Jamaican that was responsible for it is a dude named Christopher!" he told them, on the verge of tears.

"What?" Duddy screamed.

"Oh, hell naw, cuzz! Them ho's gotta pay for that shit!" D-Train chimed in.

"Yeah, cuzz, straight up. That's why I'm here, my nigga. I don't know exactly how to handle the shit. I mean I got an idea, but I want to talk to you cats about it," Julius explained, and laid out his plan to the men.

The discussion went on for what seemed like hours, and by the time Julius left he was ecstatic. The thought of taking out revenge on the men that killed his friend gave him goose bumps. It would be brutal and ruthless. The plan made him anxious. He laughed a sinister laugh as he exited the cook house and out into the night air. He was so absorbed in his thoughts of retribution that before he realized it, he had walked all the way to Angelica's house.

Chapter 25

Us Against the World

Julius felt like he had died and gone to Heaven. It seemed as though he had waited his whole life to get his chance with Angelica. They had done a little sneaking around in the past, but never had they been able to really spend time together. With Julius' grades improving and him really focusing on his studies, her mother was really starting to let them spend time together.

As an educator, Mrs. Gray was excited about the prospect of her daughter and Julius both going to college, even if it was all the way in Georgia. But at least they would have a good education. Morehouse and Spellman were excellent schools.

Julius was lying across Angelica's bed with an *Ebony* magazine. He was thumbing through the pages, lost in his own thoughts.

"Ju, do you ever think about your future and see me in it?" Angelica asked him.

149

Julius put on his most serious face, turned over to face Angelica and said in his most sincere voice, "Jelly, since the first day I saw you I've wanted you in my life. Without you I have no future, straight up." He got up and walked over to her and held her close, smelling her essence, breathing in her sexuality and wanting to touch every inch of her.

Angelica knew that Julius meant every word that he said, and she loved it when he got serious. "What if we get to Atlanta and you find somebody else; somebody who is everything that you want in a woman?" she asked jokingly.

Julius smacked his lips and laughed. "Girl, please! your ass already knows that I'm not going anywhere! I love you... well there is one woman I would fire you for," he said flatly

"Oh yeah? And who might that be, Mr. Gage?" Angelica asked, pulling him close

"Yo' Momma! Hee-hee! You know I love me some fine ass Mrs. Gray!"

Angelica hit Julius in the stomach softly and playfully pushed him back onto the bed.

"Alright girl! Don't start nothing you can't and won't finish! I don't want your momma walking in and I got your legs at 10 and 2 o'clock!" Julius said in a husky voice.

Angelica could feel his manhood starting to rise beneath his jeans. She simply began rubbing it gently and whispered in his ear, "My mom is gone with her boyfriend for the whole weekend. It's just me and you, baby!"

Julius felt like he was about to explode. His dick was throbbing and his heart was racing. He had been with Shuntae sexually, but this was different. He couldn't think straight.

Angelica had no idea what she was doing. The closest she had ever come to being with a man was watching old reruns of "Dynasty". She had played with herself while looking at pictures of Julius, and imagined what it would be like when she finally made love to him.

Julius had heard the older players in the neighborhood talking about eating pussy, but *Fuck that shit!* he thought. Eating pussy was for old niggas and white boys, and he was neither of those.

Angelica started to undress Julius. First she took off his shoes, then his pants, then his T-shirt, his boxers and socks. When she saw his dick she gasped. It was the first one she had seen in the flesh. She had seen them on late night Cinemax, and from what she had seen, Julius had a big dick. It was thick and black with veins in it, and it leaned to the left.

She stepped back and began to undress herself. She felt like a little girl compared to Julius, now that she had seen his dick. Her nipples were hard and her panties were soaked. She couldn't believe how wet she was. Her pussy was throbbing so hard that it felt like she could feel her heart beating through her clitoris.

She quickly got underneath her blanket where Julius' warm, tight body was waiting. She let her hands explore his body, and again she grabbed his dick. She wanted it inside of her. She wanted Julius to make love to her.

Julius began to touch Angelica's body also, and it was beautiful! As she was undressing he had caught a glimpse of her body. It was athletic but so soft. As he was watching her, her silhouette in the moonlight made his dick even harder.

Julius straddled Angelica, looking down into her eyes. The candlelight made her eyes even more beautiful. "Jelly, I love you so much, and if you're not ready I will understand," he said.

Angelica pulled him close to her, and in a voice full of lust she said, "I'm ready to give you all of me, baby. Just be gentle."

Julius put the head of his dick inside of Jelly. She was very tight. He was already in love with her, but this just sealed their relationship.

Angelica gasped a little bit, but when Julius pushed his meat completely inside of her, she lost her breath completely. She was lost in ecstasy, with every thrust and pump from him. Her body seemed to respond in rhythm. It felt so good that she couldn't believe that she had waited so long to give herself to him. She felt her body tingling. She was getting what seemed like hot flashes and she started to shake and couldn't control it. Then all of a sudden she felt her body explode in a rush of juices. It felt as though she was peeing on herself because she was so wet.

Then she felt Julius release inside of her. His cum was hot as it coated her insides. At that moment, she wasn't just in love with Julius, she was sprung.

All Angelica could think about was her future with her man, her lover and her best friend, Julius, as Keith Sweat sang,

"...You may be young,
But you're ready to learn..."

But first she wanted to do it again!

Chapter 26

Mexican Mafia Shit

Julius had dozed off holding Jelly. They had made love three times, and he was drained. His pager going off woke him up. It was Sleepy's number, followed by 911 so he knew it was an emergency. He used Angelicas phone to call Sleepy back. "Hello, may I speak to Sleepy, please?" he said politely to the woman on the other end of the phone.

"Okay, just one minute, please," the lady said in broken English.

Julius could hear Spanish being spoken in the background when Sleepy finally came to the phone. *"Bueno, vato,"* he said.

Julius was getting a little irritated and he only wanted to get down to business. "What up, dawg? What's the emergency?"

"I don't wanna talk on the phone. *Mi hermano,* can you come over?"

Julius thought for a minute, then said "Just meet me at my house, mane. How long will it take you to get there?"

"It should only take me fifteen, twenty minutes tops, *vato*."

"Alright, homey, I'll be there waiting for you." Julius kissed Angelica softly on her lips and she woke up. "Baby, I gotta go. I have some business to take care of. I'll call you later on tonight and check on you," Julius said, and kissed her again.

"Okay, Ju. Be careful. I love you!" Angelica was still dick-drunk, so she turned over and went back to sleep.

When Julius got home, Sleepy was already there waiting for him. "Alright, *ese*, what's so urgent?" he asked.

"We been doing these heists for a minute, and between the dope we been getting and the money we came up on, these young *miates* ain't wanting for nothing, right?" Sleepy said as to make a point.

"Yeah, you're right, so what about it?"

"Well, there's talk on the streets that some of your lil' niggas ain't satisfied with the money, homes!" Sleepy said, his irritation clearly showing.

Julius couldn't believe his ears. They had done what they set out to do. They had run the Jamaicans out of South Dallas and put money in everybody's pocket.

Out of all of the dope traps that they had kicked in they had spilled a lot of blood, but they had only lost two people, including Shy. Shy had been killed a couple months earlier, when one of the Jamaicans had recognized him as he was coming out of Little World Grocery Store. That morning he had been kidnapped and killed.

The majority of the youngsters were putting their money away like Julius had advised, but a few of them were spending like it was going out of style. Their money would be low, so it wouldn't be hard to figure out who was unhappy with their pockets.

"*Mi hermano*, listen. My uncles have some business for you, but they want to make sure your circle is tight before they get into business with you heavy," Sleepy said.

"Yeah, yeah, okay! I understand!" Julius said, obviously annoyed with the whole conversation. His mind was racing now. To be running the streets and putting family business out there was a strict no-no. Whoever was running their mouth would be dealt with severely and harshly, and he wouldn't have to touch them. Once Duddy and D-Train got the word that somebody in the clique was running their mouth about anything, the punishment would be swift and brutal. D-Train didn't talk much anyway, and he didn't have patience for those that talked at all. His philosophy was that if you would talk shit about your homies to anybody, then you wouldn't mind running your mouth and talking shit to the law.

Julius' attitude toward the whole situation was *Fuck it! If they didn't appreciate the money he had helped them make, then they wouldn't get money at all!*

Sleepy shook Julius' hand, got into his car and drove off. Julius could hear him jamming NWA. His stereo was loud, and all you could hear was Eazy E. rapping,
"*...Woke up quick at about noon,
Just thought that I had to be in Compton soon...*"

Things were changing in the neighborhood, and before Julius and the rest of South Dallas knew it, the Bloods had started moving into East Dallas the same way that the Crips had invaded South Dallas years earlier. Julius and his boys had successfully gotten rid of the Jamaicans, and now they had to worry about the Bloods coming in trying to take over territory that had primarily belonged to the Mexicans.

Months earlier after the death of Shy, Julius had put his plan into motion. He had contacted the same Jamaican that had called and told him about Christopher, and simply explained to him that if he refused to set up the Jamaican, Christopher, then he would gladly give Christoper the heads up that it was he who was trying to start a war, and that it was he who had given Julius the information that they needed to get the jump on him. Julius explained that being a Jamaican, Christopher would surely believe him, because the Jamaicans believed that all young Americans were dumb, and a plan that elaborate couldn't have been thought up without help.

After close consideration, the Jamaican had agreed, and exactly two weeks after Shy had been murdered Julius' revenge had been exacted. The older Jamaican man had convinced Christopher that the perpetrators of the robbery wanted to have a sit-down with him for fear of their lives. Christopher had pompously agreed, thinking that he would lure the youngsters into a trap and murder them all.

By the time the Jamaicans had arrived at the Silver Slipper Lounge for the meeting with the teens, Julius and his gang had already reached the club. They were in cars parked close by. They had also set explosives around the club in preparation for the arrival of the Posse. The plan was simple: The club had one way in and one way out. They would set simultaneous fires around the club and set off the explosives at the same time. Anyone exiting the club would be executed by gunfire.

The Jamaicans arrived right on schedule and filed into the club in droves. Once they were all inside, Julius and D-

Train gave the go-ahead from both sides of the club. The club erupted in a massive explosion of fireworks. The east side of the building facing Oakland Boulevard was completely demolished. A few Jamaicans had come staggering out of the Silver Slipper dazed from the explosion, and were instantly killed in a hail of rounds from AK-47's and SKS assault rifles.

It was over. The Jamaicans were gone, and the few that were left had no guidance or leadership so they were more than happy to pack up and leave, and that was that.

The East Side Locos reported directly to Sleepy's uncles. Julius already knew that when the war popped off, the Mexicans would tap the 357um Crips to help rid East Dallas of the Bloods. The way Julius felt right now, it was, *Fuck it! If the Mexicans called, then 357um would answer.* But first he had to clean house.

Chapter 27

Angelica's Dream

Angelica couldn't believe she had gone through with it. She had given her virginity to Julius, and it was beautiful. Some of her friends had told her that it would hurt and some had told her that it would feel good, but in all actuality, it hurt so good. She was really in love with Julius. He was everything that she wanted in a man.

Her mother didn't know Julius like she did. She thought she did because she had known him since he was eight or nine years old, but she didn't know shit. Angelica knew his heart, and now she knew his body.

She knew Julius had done some bad things in his life, but she also believed him when he told her that whenever he had to hurt someone, it was because they had deserved it. She saw firsthand how respectful he was to women and old people. She saw how people listened when he spoke. She saw how his voice commanded attention and respect. He was like a ghetto E.F. Hutton; when Julius spoke, everybody listened. She liked it and she wanted to be a part of it.

In her heart and mind it felt like them making love had brought them closer together. Angelica's mother didn't understand her love for Julius, and Angelica didn't feel particularly pressed to make her understand.

This was Jelly and Julius' senior year in high school, and after graduation when they were in Atlanta they could be together every day. The two of them had already discussed getting an apartment off campus. Julius had insisted on this, saying that he had more than enough money to support them both while they were in school. Jelly knew that her mother would have a problem with that, but she also realized that she would be eighteen years old and fully capable of making her own decisions.

Jelly couldn't stop thinking about Julius, his swagger, his demeanor and his cock strong attitude, but most of all the way he treated her. He was such a gentleman.

Her daydreams were interrupted by a light tap at her bedroom door. "Come in," she said softly.

It was her mother. She just stood in the doorway looking at Angelica. It was hard for the young girl to read her mother's thoughts, and for a moment she let her mind drift.

She thought about how beautiful her mother looked standing there in white Christian Dior slacks and elegant white blouse that showed just enough of her cleavage. To top it off, she wore red six-inch stiletto heels and a big red belt to compliment her outfit. She was beautiful, and Angelica just hoped that she would be half as classy and beautiful as her mother when she was her age.

"Is something wrong, Mother?" she asked, trying desperately not to let her irritation show.

"Why do you ask, dear heart? Should there be anything wrong?" Mrs. Gray asked, amused at her daughter's obvious frustration.

"No, Mother. I'm just saying, you come tapping on the door and then just stand there looking at me. I'm just trying to figure out what's going on. If you have something on your mind I wish you would just say it!" Angelica said, fuming.

Her mother frowned slightly, and then started talking slowly—almost too slowly—and deliberately to let Angelica know that she was serious. "Jelly, baby, listen. Everything I've done has been for you. I've always been totally honest with you and somewhat blunt, but always totally honest. I know that you love Julius, but I also know that you are a smart young lady. Therefore, I'm going to give you this advice. Be careful. I'm not trying to raise any more babies. If you get pregnant, Angelica, we are going to have a major problem. I need you to focus on your goals and keep your eyes on the prize!"

"Mommy, I respect you as my mother and everything that you say, but I love Julius, and our plans don't include a baby!"

Mrs. Gray smiled at her daughter. She had always thought that when they had this talk it would be under bad circumstances, but she was happy with the outcome. She hugged Angelica, kissed her on the forehead and left her only daughter alone with her thoughts.

Angelica laid in her bed thinking about what her mother had just said. That would be too ironic! If she got pregnant her first time sleeping with Julius that would be crazy. But she and Julius weren't planning on a baby so she wasn't worried.

Chapter 28

Mr. Businessman

Julius was on cloud nine. He couldn't believe that he had finally made love to Angelica. He had loved her since elementary school, and now they were seniors in high school.

Yeah, love was all fine and dandy, but it had to take a backseat right now. He was getting ready to hit the streets, and in the streets love could get you killed. All it took was for you to be sitting up daydreaming about your girl, and somebody could run up on you and catch you slipping. Julius made sure he was up on his game at all times. Plus, he had a meeting with Sleepy's uncles, and according to Sleepy they were ready to put Julius up on some life changing money, so he had to put his game face on.

Julius felt a little pressure, not about the lucrative new position offered by the Mexicans, but pressure to make as much money as possible before he graduated from high school.

Life at Lincoln High School definitely had its perks, being who he was, but Julius didn't know if he could maintain a drug empire and a college lifestyle. One thing he did know was that he wasn't trying to make a career out of selling drugs.

Another issue was the Mexicans. His boy, Sleepy was cool and he had done a little business with them, but truth be told, he didn't know them well enough to know whether they would let him out of the game. His boys would be just fine on their own, and he had soldiers that were ready to step up and do whatever he said, whether that be going to war with the Mexicans or taking over his lucrative drug operation.

Julius controlled the South Dallas drug market, and although it was only one section, it was his section. Dallas was a big city, and he made a lot of money on the streets of South Dallas.

His pager went off. He knew from the number that it was Sleepy. Whenever Sleepy wanted to get in contact with him he would always page him from the payphone outside of the warehouse that Julius sometimes used. He called Sleepy from the payphone in front of the Chinese store. "What's up, *vato*?" he asked when Sleepy answered the phone.

"What's happening, *ese*? My uncles are sending a car for you, homes. They're eager to get shit cracking."

"Alright, mane. I'm in front of the Chinese store on Dixon, waiting on these lil' niggas to bring me my money. Then it's whatever with me, dawg," Julius told him, then hung up the phone.

Julius was still standing in front of the store when a couple of his soldiers rode up in a black Monte Carlo with tan interior, and sitting on gold Daytona 100 spoke rims. The car was nice, but he didn't understand why his homeboys would buy cars that they really had no business driving, because they were too young get a driver's license. Most of them didn't have so much as a learner's permit. The cars were too fancy, and they would only draw heat and could be potentially fatal, because if the jack boys didn't get you and make you a victim, then you were a constant target of the Dallas Police Department, more specifically the Gang Task Force. It had two officers that were as crooked as they were relentless. "Mr. Mustache" and his partner, "Cigar" were crooked cops that had a reputation for being merciless to the young gang bangers in the neighborhood. They were assholes to anybody who had ties to a gang, and that was basically everybody in South Dallas under the age of twenty five years old.

"What up, big homey? Let me holla at 'cha, mane," the driver of the Monte Carlo called out to him.

Julius walked over and stuck his head in the window. Leaning in, he said, "Is everything here, mane? This is the money from all three houses?"

All three men in the car nodded in agreement.

"Yeah, Ju, man, you already know what it is with us, homey. Trey fi' seven fo' life, my nigga! Shit, we ain't gonna ever steal from you or the set, cuzz!" the thug in the back seat said.

"Yeah, I hear you, lil' homey. I was just asking," Julius responded.

The passenger handed Julius a brown Kroger paper sack full of money.

"Okay, mane. Baldhead Tashia's gonna drop y'all some shit off later, cuzz," Julius said.

As he stood up and looked around, he saw a Limousine pulling into the parking lot of the store. He thought that it might be the Mexicans, but he wasn't certain.

Then a tall Mexican in a black suit emerged from the driver's side and beckoned Julius over to him. As Julius approached, he extended his hand to the tall man and asked, "What's up, bro? Who are you looking for?"

"I'm looking for a *vato* named Julius, homes," the Mexican stated.

"Yeah, that's me. Were you sent by the Barrera's?"

The driver just nodded as he opened the door for him.

When Julius stepped into the Limousine, he was surprised that Michael and Antonio Barrera were already inside waiting for him. He smiled to himself, thinking that every time he saw the brothers they were dressed like they had just stepped out of an episode of "Miami Vice". Julius liked it. He thought that it made them look like money.

Mike Barrera was the older brother. He had a dark complexion and salt and pepper hair, and a salt and pepper goatee. He sported a white linen suit with a peach colored shirt underneath. Julius also noticed that he had on expensive alligator sandals.

The younger of the two brothers was Flaco, and he had on a camel colored pants and shirt set and his shoes were also alligator, but the pattern was a lot bigger and they looked more expensive. His complexion was equally as dark, but his hair was jet black, and he was clean cut with no facial hair.

Just being in their presence, Julius felt like he had to step his game up even more.

The older brother noticed Julius admiring their clothes and took the opportunity to break the silence. He spoke

166

with obvious intelligence, and his Spanish accent was almost unrecognizable. "Young Julius, we have watched you closely. By the way you do business and the way that the streets respect you, we need a man like that in our organization."

Julius thought carefully and then stated flatly, "All of that sounds good, sir, but I need you to understand before I make any kind of commitment, that I do not plan on being a career drug dealer. I plan on walking away from this life one day."

The younger man smiled at him. When he spoke, Julius noticed that his English was bad, but still good enough to be understood. "*Ese*, we have no intentions of tying you into a situation that you don't want to be a part of. If the time ever arises when you no longer want this opportunity, all you have to do is say the word."

The older brother continued. "We want to give you an opportunity to come in and make some serious money. If you take this opportunity that we are presenting to you and follow the blueprint that we are going to lay out for you, I guarantee that by the time you graduate from high school this year I will have made you a millionaire!" Mike Barrera said.

Julius was making some good money with his little operation, but the way the Barrera's were talking, they wanted Julius to have his hands in some heavy shit. In no uncertain terms they had made it clear that they wanted to make him the king of the Dallas drug trade. He would go from a six figure nigga to a seven or eight figure nigga in a few short months.

They invited him to their home in Highland Park. Highland Park was an affluent neighborhood in the suburb of North Dallas, and it was a neighborhood with million dollar homes, with manicured lawns in plush, gated communities.

As they were pulling up to a mansion, Julius looked out of the window of the Limousine, and the first thing he saw was the huge wrought iron gate with the letters "MB" on it. He also noticed that you had to pass through a security checkpoint to get onto the property.

The security guard was obviously Mexican, and he carried an AK47 automatic rifle. He examined the driver and then walked around to the back door of the Limo. The window came down, and he looked inside the car and gave Mr. Barrera a nod. Even though the man recognized the car, it was still a security measure to check and make sure that it was really the brothers.

Once they entered the property, Julius was awestruck by the giant statues of white lions that lined both sides of the driveway leading up to the main house. The house was huge. It was the kind of house you only saw on television, and he was thoroughly impressed.

Inside the house, the brothers lead Julius to a huge dining hall. Inside the dining hall there was a long glass and marble table, and around the table sat sixteen men, all of whom were either Mexican or Caucasian.

A tall white man stood and said, "Welcome, young Julius. It is indeed a pleasure to meet you. I am Judge Wilkinson."

Each man followed suit with introductions. As they introduced themselves, they also included their titles and the roles that they played. It seemed as though each man's title was just as impressive as the next. There were lawyers present to take care of everything, from traffic tickets to murder cases. There were doctors there so you never had to go to the hospital and put people in your business. There were bank managers there to launder whatever money was made. Of course Judge Wilkinson, and another judge by the name of Judge Deets. And then there were the Barrera Cartel members. Only the head men were present at this meeting. Sleepy arrived, and he joined the meeting.

Mike Barrera signaled that it was time to get down to business. "Julius, the reason we have called you here today, or better yet the reason we chose to bring you into our organization, is simple. You have cornered a market that none of us can go after. Every man here plays a role in how we do things. We have always wanted into that market, but we wanted to use someone that we felt confident we could trust. We are going to take the southern states by storm, and you, young man, will spearhead this movement. Julius, we have been working with a group of chemists to develop a marriage of sorts." He paused to let his words sink in.

What Mr. Barrera was proposing wasn't unheard of. It was, however, risky and very expensive.

"The only thing we need to know is when and where, *Tio Miguel*," Sleepy said.

Nobody responded. They merely looked at Sleepy as to say, "Shut the fuck up!"

Mr. Barrera just shook his head, obviously embarrassed for his young nephew. He walked between Sleepy and Julius, put his arms around each teenager's shoulder, lowered his voice down to a deadly whisper and said, "Sleepy, the way you think will keep you from reaching your full potential. You love to rush into things blindly. Julius, on the other hand, takes all of the pieces, puts them together and weighs his options, and *then* acts.

This is a quality that you had better learn fast if you intend to make it out of this thing alive, *pinche' panzon!*" Mr. Barrera was irritated, but he still seemed to be in good spirits.

Julius looked at the older man closely and said, "Mr. Barrera, may I ask you a question, sir?"

"Of course, Julius. You may ask whatever you wish."

"Sir, what exactly do we need a chemist for? I know how to cook up cocaine."

Mr. Barrera began to laugh almost uncontrollably. "No, young Julius. This is not the reason we have employed chemists. We wanted to utilize every aspect of the dope trade. As you know we control cocaine, marijuana and heroin. With the chemists we are going to create the perfect drug; the ultimate high!"

All of the men in the room began to talk amongst themselves. This was the first they had heard of this.

What the Barrera's were proposing would make everyone involved rich beyond their wildest dreams. They would combine a quarter kilo of heroin to every kilo of cocaine, effectively making speedballs. Unknown to the street level dealer, the fiends would get the high from the cocaine, and the sickness from the heroin. If they tried to get their dope from someone other than the people working for Julius and the Barrera's, the ordinary crack wouldn't stop them from being dope sick.

Julius took in every word, knowing that it would not only create an unheard of revenue stream, but it would also bring a new line of enemies that he would have to prepare for. Niggas get violent when they get hungry, and if the new drug dried up their money, the dealers would either have to get on board or starve; either get down or lay down; roll with them or get rolled over!

Chapter 29

¿Soy de Familia? No le

Sleepy was making damn good money, but he knew that things were about to get even better. His uncles were happy with the way Julius hustled, and they were constantly telling Sleepy what a good find he had been. Plus, he and Julius had a couple of afterhours spots set up around town, so that was extra money too.

However, the one thing that Sleepy couldn't shake was the fact that his uncles seemed to have more love for Julius than their own flesh and blood. They put Julius before him when they made decisions, and his uncles had asked him pointblank if it made him jealous. He had lied and said no, but truth of the matter was that it ate at him all the time.

But Sleepy was a gangster's gangster. As far as he was concerned, they could marry the *pinche' miate'* as long as he kept getting paid. He had made so much money that he was considering going to Mexico with his grandparents, finding a little *chabala*, buying a ranch and settling down. But he already knew from experience that his uncles would never let that happen.

Sleepy sat on the giant white plush sofa in his uncles' massive den and watched as his uncle escorted Julius into his office and closed the door.

Julius stepped inside the office and was immediately shocked by the number of books Mr. Barrera had. On every wall of the office there were large cherry wood bookshelves that reached from floor to ceiling. He had never seen so many books outside of a library.

In the center of the office sat an oversized cherry wood desk that was identical to the texture and color of the bookshelves. On the massive desk sat a briefcase made of ostrich skin. It smelled expensive in the office, like wood and new money.

Mr. Barrera walked around the desk and sat in his high-backed leather "king's throne". He motioned for Julius to take a seat across from him.

Julius did as he was told and tried hard to focus. There was so much to think about, but he wanted and needed to pay attention. There were many questions that he wanted to ask, but he was also intelligent enough and business savvy enough to know that it was better to just listen sometimes. If he played his cards right with the Mexicans, he would be entering college a very wealthy young man.

Mr. Barrera leaned back in his chair, admiring the young man. He was a certified hustler, and his mind stayed on his money. Mr. Barrera liked that about Julius. He could also be an identical twin to his father, Julius Sr.

Mike Barrera had met Julius Sr. in his early days when the Barrera brothers were just starting to earn a reputation in the streets. During that period in time, certain names rang like Christmas bells, and the Gage brothers' names rang the loudest. They were primed to rule the streets in Texas and abroad.

Julius Sr. was charismatic, suave, aggressive, and most importantly ruthless. He and Mike Barrera had been more like business associates than friends, but nevertheless he'd held a fondness for Julius Sr. and they shared a mutual respect.

Julius Sr. and his brother, Charlie Boy were some of their best customers. When they met, the Gage brothers were buying at least five pounds of weed a week from the Barrera brothers, and all of the stolen liquor they could supply. Occasionally the Barrera's had even used Julius for muscle.

Now here it was years later, and he had the pleasure of doing business with his son. When Sleepy had told his uncle about the cool black dude he was locked up with, his name immediately rang a bell.

Mike Barrera got up and stood up behind his leather king's throne and began to pace nervously back and forth behind his desk. He was a coldblooded kingpin, but he also had a heart, and telling his young protégé how and why his father was murdered was going to be hard. Telling him *who* murdered his father would be one of the most difficult things he had ever done. "Young Julius, you are a very smart young man, and there are things that I need to tell you before we take our business relationship any further," he began.

Julius was all ears. He didn't think there was anything that could hinder his campaign of getting money, but nevertheless he gave Mr. Barrera his undivided attention.

"Julius, I knew your father. He was a very important man in the Dallas underworld. Your father helped a lot of people in South Dallas, so a lot of people loved him. But for every person that loved him, there were two that hated him. They hated him because of his success, and they hated him because they feared him. Your father always said that he would rather be feared than loved, but that same fear had bred hatred and contempt and it cost him his life."

Julius' head was spinning. The only thing that he had heard about his father's death was that his father was murdered. There had never been an explanation of who or why, only a where it happened. He knew that his father had been murdered in Dixon Circle, but he hadn't heard much else. He was dazed and a little confused. *Was Mr. Barrera trying to tell me who did it? Was he trying to tell me how and why it happened?*

"Young Julius, the men that murdered your father, your Uncle Charlie and your Aunt Pearl are still alive. For many years I contemplated whether I should just eliminate the threat for you as a courtesy to your father, but then my paternal instincts took over. There was no way I was prepared to deprive you the opportunity to avenge your family's deaths. The way your family died was brutal and vicious. In this business it sometimes comes like that, but Pearl's murder was senseless, and for that they must pay. What I'm about to tell you is going to test your soul as a man, and it's also going to send you on an emotional rollercoaster. But before I tell you, I need your word as a man; I need you to make me a promise."

Julius' blood was boiling. He had to know, and he was damn near ready to sell his soul to find out.

Chapter 30

What's Done in the Dark

Najé had just gotten home from shopping at Sound Warehouse. She bought some new records. She was eager to put on the new Whitney Houston so she could do some thinking while she cleaned. She was about to go into her bedroom and show her husband what she'd bought, but she stopped in her tracks because she heard Booty Green talking.

"Mane, listen. The only reason that little muthafucka is still alive is because I love his mammy. 'Nuff said!"

The conversation went on and on, and the things her husband said about her son, his father and his past made Najé cringe. He had basically incriminated himself and whoever else was on the other end of the phone, but she wasn't the police; she was a mother. She was torn, and for once in her life she didn't know what to do or what to say. All she really knew is that she had to keep her son safe; that was her first priority. She had to warn Julius. She didn't know what she would do about Mr. Booty Green, but Julius was what mattered.

Najé didn't know how much Julius knew about this current revelation, but one thing was certain; he was his father's son through and through, so when he found out the bullshit that she had just found out, there was going to be smoke in the city. She thought that the best way to communicate with her son was through pen and paper. Julius always responded positively to his her writings, and this time it was definitely needed.

In her heart she felt like Julius already knew everything, so she would craft her letter accordingly. If he didn't know what she was talking about, he would ask. If he already knew, then the letter she had planned for him would hit home and make a statement. There would be plenty of time to deal with Mr. Booty Green. Julius' heart and wellbeing had to be guarded above all else. She sat down to compose her letter:

My baby son:

Julius, you are loved. Yes, you are loved, but more importantly, you yourself are love.

No matter how much hatred and recrimination you have stuffed down inside of yourself for the people that killed your father, you are still love. Anybody who knows what love is doesn't need a reason or permission to love. It's one of those feelings that flare up like a rocket (once you let go and really love). The flare from the rocket bursts into the atmosphere and melts there. The body of the rocket drops to the ground to be recycled or thrown on a trash heap. But what came from it cannot be seen, retrieved or reused. It just lingers. That's power. Sounds foolish?

Love doesn't need a reason to shower itself on the world. Hatred is bent on destroying love because it (hatred) knows that love cannot, will not and does not exist, or co-exist with hatred. And hatred knows it has no purpose. To love is to let go of past hurts, disappointments, anger and hatred. Hatred knows this and it hangs on for dear life.

You might wonder why I'm speaking of hatred as if they are people. They reside in us people as spirits. I want you to be free from hatred, baby boy. Free to make wise decisions in all you do. Just as we feed our bodies to maintain wellness, we must also feed our spirits with the food of love. Love is not an easy food to swallow because we have to give up our "isms"; we have to give up our "fuck you" vacations that pay us absolutely nothing but fear and anger. We as people have a lot of negative "isms" that really don't give a shit about our spiritual wellness or serve a purpose.

I don't want you to seek vengeance, but if you must seek your own vengeance just know that I love you very much, and I want you to be smart. It's easy to get into trouble, and oh so very hard to get out of it, Julius. Be wise, be safe, and be love. Your destiny is in your own hands, and nobody can or should be able to dictate your future.

I love you, my son.

Mommy.

After she finished the letter, Najé left home, headed for Dixon Circle in search of her youngest son. When she found him they would have to close this chapter of their lives, pick up the pieces and move on. They would be okay. They always had been and always would be.

Chapter 31

Red Rum

Mr. Barrera studied his young protégé. Julius was visibly shaken, and Mr. Barrera could tell that the young man's curiosity was eating away at him.

In a low and measured tone, Julius began to speak. "Mr. Barrera, with all due respect, sir, I just want to hear it. I want to know what happened and who killed my father." He had tears in his eyes and his head was pounding. His heart was heavy with memories of his father.

"Julius, this will be a difficult pill to swallow for you, but if you feel you need to know, my friend, I want to share this information with you. I will keep it simple and to the point."

"There were three men and one woman directly responsible for your father's death. The woman's name was Chele, and she died after your father but before your uncle. She killed herself because the guilt of what she'd done to your father was unbearable, and the guilt led her to suicide.
"

"The men responsible for your father's death are men that are close to you, Julius; men you may or may not have grown to love. The man you know as Uncle Rabbit, the pimp, Yellow Shoes, and your stepfather, Booty Green killed your father, your Uncle Charles and your Aunt Pearl."

"Booty Green's mission was to get close enough to your mother so that he could get you alone and eliminate you as a threat. But he fell in love with Najé. That's the only reason you're still alive."

Julius was furious and he was confused. He began to worry about his mother. If Booty Green and his boys had murdered his father, uncle and aunt, they wouldn't hesitate to murder his mother.

Mr. Barrera, as if reading the young man's mind, said firmly, "I believe your mother is in danger, Julius, so I'm sending men to keep an eye on her as we speak. Whatever you decide to do concerning this situation, young man, just know that you have my full support. Whatever you need is only a phone call away."

Julius left Mr. Barrera's mansion in the back of the Limousine, alone, dazed and livid. Hatred coursed through his veins, and the three men responsible for his father's death would pay heavily for it. They had made a fool of him.

He also began to wonder whether his mother knew and just hadn't told him, or whether Booty Green suspected that his mother knew. Julius reasoned that he couldn't know, because she would probably be dead if he had any idea.

He needed to talk to someone, he needed to vent, but most of all he needed to make sense of the bullshit he'd just learned.

He signaled the Limousine driver and gave him Angelicas address. Angelica always listened and she never judged. She would know what to do. He needed her levelheaded thinking right now, because the way he was feeling was irrational.

The more Julius thought about it, the angrier he got. How could this muthafucka look him in his eyes every day, knowing what he had done? Maybe Green felt guilty, and that was why he always tried to be so cool with him. Well, guilt wouldn't save his life. The thought of all of the good times he had had with the man responsible for murdering his family was almost unbearable.

He didn't give a fuck about Booty Green, but he did love his mother. He didn't want to hurt her, but her husband had to go for what he'd done to his father and family. He wouldn't tell her of his knowledge, because he knew she loved her husband and he didn't want to break her heart.

The Limo pulled up in front of Angelica's house just before dark. Julius was relieved to see that her mother was not at home. He used the telephone inside of the car to call Angelica. She answered on the first ring.

"Hello."

"Hey, baby, I'm outside. Open the door."

Angelica looked out through her living room blinds and saw Julius exiting a snow-white Lincoln Continental. He looked shaken and uneasy. He looked around nervously as he moved up the sidewalk. Even in his shaken state, he was still the most handsome chocolate man she had ever seen. Whatever his problem was, she was sure he would share it with her. He always did.

When Julius made it to the front door, Angelica was standing in the doorway, and Toney Toni Tone's "Relax" playing in the background. When she hugged him she could feel him trembling. He looked as though he had just seen a ghost, and she could feel his heartbeat through his T-shirt. It was going to be a long night.

Chapter 32

Don't Get Nervous Now

Booty Green had stopped talking because he thought
he'd heard someone eaves dropping on his conversation.
He got out of the tub and wrapped one of the many plush
Neiman Marcus towels around his waist. He found his wife
in the home office typing on the computer. He didn't
disturb her because he knew from experience that when she
was typing she didn't like to be disturbed, so he went to the
bar and fixed her an E & J and Coke, took it to her, kissed
her on the cheek and left her alone.

Booty Green had no idea that Najé had overheard his
conversation. She had heard his treachery. He had no idea
that his beautiful wife was typing his death warrant.

Booty Green dressed slowly while thinking about how
good life was. He had money in the bank, a beautiful wife, a
good stepson and a good friend. He was changing his life
for the better, slowly but surely. He would let the past stay
in the past. He had buried it, and if he could keep it buried

he could continue to live his life as he saw fit. Anybody that got in his way would be dealt with swiftly and harshly.

******

As Najé drove toward Dixon Circle, her mind was racing. Julius was her youngest child and she felt a certain need to protect him from any and all dangers that he might face. She loved her husband, but she would kill him dead before she let him lay a hand on her baby. Her maternal instincts were in overdrive.

Julius only had a few weeks until graduation, and the way that his friends had been getting killed, she knew that his graduating was a big cause for celebration. She hadn't bothered to drink the E & J that Green gave her. She didn't trust him, and she wasn't sure if she ever would again.

******

Booty Green drove on I-35 headed towards Oak Cliff, wondering what was so urgent. Yellow Shoes had paged him "911", and when Green had called him he'd flatly told him, "We need to talk."

As he approached Yellow Shoes' house, he saw Rabbit pulling in. Although they were all good friends, the urgency with which Yellow Shoes called set Green's wheels turning, and to see Rabbit there served as proof that something was wrong. They never really discussed any of the dirt that they had done together, because they had an unspoken understanding: *Why talk about what they all knew anyway?*

Green was worried because although he was powerful in his own right, both Rabbit and Yellow Shoes had major street cred. Ever since he married Najé, he'd been out of the loop. He still maintained relationships, but the majority of his time was spent trying to build a family.

Green pulled into the circular driveway and parked his new Eldorado. He could hear Johnny Taylor blaring from somewhere inside the house:

> *"...Who's making love to yo' old lady,*
> *While you're out making love..."*

Even though Booty Green trusted his wife completely, he couldn't help but to think of her when he heard that song. Johnny Taylor was her favorite blues artist. Every Saturday he would be awakened by the sounds of Johnny Taylor and the smell of Pine-sol. His wife had the same routine every weekend. She would open every window in the house, put on her music, and clean house from top to bottom.

Rabbit hopped out of his Lincoln Continental, smoking a pipe. It was funny because he never smoked tobacco in the pipe, only weed, and it was always the strongest weed. He walked over and slapped Green on his back as he got out of his Cadillac. "What's up, playa?" he asked Green.

"Slow boogie, baby!" Green replied.

"Yeah, mane, slow motion is better than no motion!" Rabbit countered.

Green just ignored the statement, wanting to cease with the small talk. "So, what's this meeting all about anyway, buddy?" he asked.

"Aw, man, you know how that nigga Yellow Shoes is. No worries, mane," Rabbit reassured his friend.

The pair of gangsters walked into Yellow Shoes' house, and the smell of weed and incense filled the air.

Yellow Shoes was sitting at his dining room table. He was dressed like a classic pimp, in a long red blazer suit with gold pinstripes, a red silk shirt, a yellow silk tie, a red Dobbs fedora with a yellow band, and his signature yellow alligator shoes. He had the lights turned down low and yellow candles lit. The darkness with the candles cast an eerie glow over him as he sat alone. "Come in, playas... come in," he gestured. "Can I get you cats anything to drink?"

"Yeah, lemme get a Crown and Coke," Rabbit said.

Shoes looked at Green. "How about you? You drankin?" he asked flatly.

"Yellow Shoes, you've known me long enough to know what I drank, mane. What's with the formal shit, playa?" Green asked, obviously irritated.

"Okay, E & J and Coke it is," Shoes said.

Yellow Shoes motioned to one of the many naked young ladies walking around. "C'mere, bitch! Bring my playa podnas a couple dranks. Brang Booty Green E & J and Coke, and Rabbit a Crown and Coke, and hurry up ho!" he stated smoothly, the words flowing from his mouth like nothing.

The young girl, who couldn't be any older than nineteen, just smiled shyly and disappeared into the kitchen. As she walked away, Rabbit couldn't help but notice how tight her body was. She was about 5'2", had a light brown complexion like a Puerto Rican, had green eyes and flowing jet black hair. She was built like a track star, and Rabbit felt his manhood start to rise. "Yellow Shoes, mane, you got these little bad bitches running round this bitch like a nigga's blind. You need to tell dat lil' bitch,

Ebony to put a nigga in it!" he said half joking and half serious.

"Number one, nigga, you know the game. The bitches in my presence is about a dollar, so you gotta break bread. And number two, you my partner, and I don't wanna fall out with you over my bitches. Now, let's get down to business, playas," Yellow Shoes stated.

Booty Green was growing tired and irritated with the runaround game. He was just ready to know what could possibly be so urgent.

Yellow Shoes sat there looking at his two closest friends. Life was about family and good friends, but it was first and foremost about self-preservation. But as much love as he had for his friends, he wasn't willing to die or go to prison for them.

Booty Green had to be dealt with. Shoes would give him an opportunity to make things right, but that opportunity wouldn't be afforded to him for long. Their past was catching up to them fast, and Shoes was almost certain that Green was unaware of what was going on. Love had a way of blinding you like that.

Yellow Shoes had to pick his words carefully. His friend was volatile and violent, and even though he didn't fear him, he still knew him well enough to not want any problems with him if they could be avoided. "Booty Green, I've known you for a gang of years, mane, and I done always shot straight with you, so I'm telling you this as a friend, playa. You slippin'."

Booty Green was trying to keep an open mind, but he felt like he was being attacked. "And what's that shit supposed to mean, mane?" he asked.

Rabbit, trying to diffuse the situation, chimed in. "Booty, mane, we all know that you went into this thang with Najé to get close enough to keep an eye on that little nigga, and yo' ass fell in love with that bitch!" Rabbit barked.

"Hold up, mothafucka! That's my fuckin' wife you speakin' on, nigga!" Booty Green replied

"See, this is the shit I'm talking about. You done forgot what's at stake, nigga. Are you that much in love, playa?" Shoes asked. He was sympathetic to his friend, because he knew that Green really loved Najé, but he also knew that when the shit hit the fan, it could easily get out of hand.

"Listen, Booty Green. This is very important. I need—"

Just as Shoes was about to finish his sentence the doorbell rang. One of his little young broads answered the door, and walked the guest into the dining room.

Green couldn't believe his eyes. Why was his stepson's friend here? The young Mexican, Sleepy walked in and gave a nervous nod to all of the men present.

"Sleepy, come on in, youngster. You want a drink?" Shoes offered.

"Naw, homes, I'm okay right now," Sleepy said. He noticed Booty Green and Rabbit looking at him with disgust. Yeah, Julius was supposed to be his friend, but that's not how he felt. He felt betrayed because his own uncles seemed to love Julius more than him. *Fuck Julius! Pinche' miate'! is how Sleepy felt. Fuck Booty Green and Rabbit too if they didn't like him.* With Julius out of the way his uncles would have no choice but to give him the opportunities that they gave Julius. He had tried unsuccessfully to get Julius killed when he had tipped off the Jamaicans as to who was responsible for the robberies of their dope houses. The Jamaicans hadn't been smart enough to eliminate Julius though, and in turn had been eliminated themselves.

Now he was facing the men that could possibly get rid of him. Sleepy was playing a dangerous game, and he knew it. If Julius' stepfather chose to tell him, then Sleepy knew that Julius wouldn't rest until he was a dead man. Sleepy gambled on the fact that after overhearing the conversation that Julius had with his uncles, he wouldn't want to hear anything that Booty Green had to say.

"Okay, young playa, I want you to tell Booty Green and Rabbit what you told me. Tell 'em everything, mane," Yellow Shoes said.

Booty Green couldn't begin to imagine what it was about, but he was eager to know.

Sleepy began to speak, telling the men how his uncles had known Julius Sr. and his family, and how they knew that the three men sitting in that room had been responsible for the murders of the Gage brothers. He also told them how his uncles had told Julius the whole story.

By the time Sleepy was done, Booty Green's head was swimming and his stomach was twisted in knots. In his eyes this was some treacherous shit that shit you only see on TV. He was torn between his love for his wife and his hatred for Julius Jr., and he was torn between his loyalty to his wife and his loyalty for his friends. Plus, he didn't know what Julius would do with the information. Would he go to the police? Would he tell his mother? Would he try and take revenge? Whatever the case, Booty Green couldn't allow him to fuck up everything he had worked for. Julius needed to be dealt with.

Sleepy collected the $5,000 from Yellow Shoes that he had been promised for the information. Sleepy didn't care about the money because he had plenty of it. What he was most concerned about was Julius' elimination.

The tension in the room was so thick you could see it floating in the air. Every man there was lost in his own thoughts.

Chapter 33

All I Got

Angelica could sense that something was wrong with Julius. He didn't look right and he wasn't acting like himself. She loved Julius with all her heart. It was almost as if they were connected, like a mother and a child. Even before he got there she knew that he wasn't well. She could feel it.

But she also knew her man well enough to know that he would just withdraw if she pressed him. She would have to wait until he was ready to share.

Julius was sitting on Angelica's bed with his head buried in his hands. He had a lot on his mind. There were only two people in the whole world he felt that he could trust. One of them was sitting across from him, and the other person was his mother. He wanted to tell Angelica what he'd found out, but he didn't know how to. She had already accepted so much in dealing with him, and he didn't want to keep burdening her with his problems. She had grown into such a beautiful young lady, and he loved her so much that he only wanted to make her happy. He loved her more than life itself, but he also wanted to protect her. His was an inner conflict, because he always told her everything. But what he wanted to do and was about to do, he was sure she wouldn't agree.

He could feel Angelica watching him, so he raised his head and she was kneeling in front of him.

She met his gaze, placed his head in her soft hands and stared into her his eyes. "Ju, baby, I want you to know that no matter what, you can always talk to me about it. No stress, no strain. I love you, and I want you to feel free to talk about any and everything with me, okay, Daddy?" she said softly.

Julius knew Angelica meant every word, and he had every intention of telling her everything and sharing his plans, but he was trying to find the right words to explain the situation. He decided that, fuck it! He would go straight at it. Angelica knew him well enough to read between the lines, he reasoned. "Jelly, baby, what I'm about to tell you will probably blow your mind like it did mine, but you hafta know it," he said.

Angelica knew it was serious, because Julius hadn't called her "Jelly" in years.

"Baby, I found out who killed my father n'em! I found out who did it and why!"

Angelica was stunned and speechless.

Julius continued, "Yeah, baby. And guess who the fuck did it?"

She could only manage to mutter and almost inaudible, "Who?"

"My step-daddy, that nigga, Rabbit and Yellow Shoes, baby!" The more he talked, the more furious he became. He had begun to raise his voice and quickly composed himself.

"For real? Damn, baby! That's fucked up! I really don't know what to say. Wow!"

"Yeah, baby, me neither. I'm fucked up in the head behind this shit, man. I got too much on my plate to have to deal with this bullshit, baby, straight up." Julius sighed.

"What are you going to do, Daddy?" she asked him.

"Oh, you already know I gots to get mine. Them niggas got to go, baby!" Julius barked.

Angelica looked at Julius and knew that he was dead serious. "Baby, I'm with you for real! If it was you or my mother, I would do the same thing!" she spat.

Julius couldn't believe his ears. He had to smile inside. His baby was trying to be a little gangster. He just looked at her and said, "Oh yeah? Ha-ha! You're a little gangsta now, huh?" He was amused.

"Hell yeah, Daddy! I couldn't imagine going through any shit like that. You and my momma are all I have. I'd bust a cap in a nigga ass 'bout mine!"

Julius and Angelica both laughed at her attempt to sound gangster. He felt a lot better now that he knew she was in his corner. "Where's your momma at anyway, Jelly?" he asked.

"I'm not sure, baby. There's no telling. Why?" asked Angelica

Instead of answering, Julius began to undress.

Angelica's panties got moist, and she giggled that uncomfortable laugh of love sick teenage girl.

She and Julius had been doing it on the regular since the first time, and even though it still hurt a little, she was getting better at taking the dick. They had also experimented with different positions. She was addicted to Julius' dick. He was turning her into a freak, and she liked it. She had also been sneaking and watching late night porn on Cinemax. She couldn't get enough of him, and she played with herself on a regular. She couldn't help herself, and now Julius was right in front of her, naked, with his muscular chocolate body glistening under the light of her bedroom lamp.

When he entered her she came instantly. Julius felt her juices, but he was getting to the point that he could hold his nut almost for as long as he wanted.

Angelica began to throw it back in rhythm with him, and felt another wave of excitement building. Julius was feeling it too. They both came together in an orgasmic explosion.

Julius collapsed on the side of her and just stared at her beautiful face in the darkness.

"What are you thinking about, baby?" she asked.

"I'm thinking about how much I love you, baby. I want you to know that if anything happens to me, you will be well taken care of. Before I do what I gotta do, I'm going to make you a list. This list will have the locations of all the places I've hidden my money. Also, it will have the contacts for my workers and connects; who owes what, and so forth and so on," Julius said confidently.

"Okay, but nothing is going to happen to you. You're too smart. Just keep in mind that we graduate in a few weeks, and we're leaving for college in the fall. Atlanta will be good for us, baby."

"I know, and I can't wait!" he said excitingly.

Julius felt as though a weight had been lifted from his shoulders. Angelica was his best friend, his lover and his everything, so to be able to tell her everything cleared his mind. Now all he had to do was plan, plot and strategize. It was going down. He would have to do it alone, because a dead man couldn't talk, and he wasn't going to snitch on himself!

Chapter 34

Face the Muzik

Najé had driven to a few of her son's known hangouts, and he wasn't at any of them. She was trying desperately not to worry, but she needed to find him before her husband did. Her husband had a reputation in South Dallas, and there was no telling what Booty Green was capable of doing to her and Julius. She also knew her son very well. He was his father's son in every way, and she knew that he would not hesitate to murder Booty Green in the name of revenge.

Najé didn't want to see her son throw away his life for her husband, who had obviously been lying to her all along. She had anger and hatred building up inside of her, but at the same time she had an amazing calm. She smirked at the irony. *How could anyone have a calm hatred?*

She decided that the best thing to do would be to go home and wait for her son. Whenever he decided to come home she would tell him, and they would have to come to terms on what their next move was going to be. By no means did she want to go into hiding, but protecting Julius was her main and only concern.

Najé's other children were scattered around and were being raised by aunts, or were already adults. A lot of people would probably pass judgment on her, saying that she wasn't a good mother, but she didn't give a damn. She lived her life believing that her children deserved to make their own decisions and their own mistakes. So when her children wanted to stay with relatives, in her mind it was all good.

As Najé pulled into her driveway she noticed that the light in the living room was on. Booty Green's car wasn't there so it had to be Julius. Her heart began to pound almost uncontrollably. She wasn't looking forward to telling her son that her husband was responsible for his father's death. She also wasn't looking forward to the hurt and pain that it was going to cause her son. She walked into her house not absolutely certain of how the outcome would be, but she didn't see where she had a choice.

Julius was standing by one of the windows, looking out. "Hey, Ma," he greeted her.

"Hey, baby."

"We need to talk," they both said at the same time.

Najé looked at her son. He looked upset and like he'd been crying, as if he already knew what the deal was. "What do you want to talk about, baby?" she asked him, almost certain that she already knew.

"Mama, I love you with everything in me, God knows I do, so believe me when I tell you it's killing me to have to tell you this... but Booty Green, Yellow Shoes and Rabbit killed my father, my uncle Charlie, and my auntie Aunt Pearl!" Julius exclaimed.

"I know, baby. I—"

Before Najé could finish her sentence Julius cut her off. "You knew this nigga killed my father and you didn't say shit? Are you siding with this nigga over me?" he spat.

"Julius, I just found out today. He was on the phone talking and he didn't know I was listening. I've been riding around looking for you all day, baby. I'm your mother before anything else. That means I'm your Mama before I'm his wife!" she said sincerely.

"I know, Ma. My head is just messed up."

"I'm sure, but I need you to be smart and be strong. Don't throw your life away for this asshole!" Najé pleaded.

"Oh, I'm not, Ma. This is going to be simple," Julius said with a smirk.

"I won't try to stop you from doing whatever it is you are going to do. I also don't want to know what you are going to do, baby boy."

Julius hugged his mother tightly. If things went according to his plans, then they would walk away free and clear.

He walked into his bedroom, tears still burning his eyes. His heart hurt and he didn't know what to do about it. But what he did know was that the men responsible for the death of his family members would pay, and they would pay in blood.

Julius sat on the edge of his bed looking around his room and trying to find some type of peace in his small space.

In his closet underneath some clothes he caught a glimpse of the safe that had been left to him by his father. He ran over to the closet and threw the clothes off of the safe, and stared at it in awe. He tried to remember the combination, but his mind was clouded. "Think, Julius!" he said to himself.

Julius frantically moved around his room, lifting mattresses and opening drawers. He went from the dresser to the nightstand, and from the nightstand to desk drawers.

The young man stopped and chuckled to himself, because he could hear his father's voice:

"Everything has a place, and every place has a thing."

Julius always hated hearing that when he was young, but it rang true. He needed to start being more organized.

He stopped, took a deep breath and tried to think. He couldn't remember the last time that he had even had the combination, and for that matter, he couldn't remember if he had ever had the combination. He was about to ask his mother, but thought better of it. If there was something in the safe that his mother didn't agree with him having, she might just try and take it.

There were only three things that Julius still had that had belonged to his father: the safe, his father's Bible, and his father's favorite watch that Julius wore every day. It was a beautiful solid gold watch encrusted with diamonds and made by Bulgari. The fit was a little big, but he loved the look of it because it was expensive, and because it belonged to his father.

Julius sat down again on the edge of the bed. He reached up on the bookshelf above his bed and grabbed his father's Bible. He quickly flipped through the pages, hoping that a piece of paper with the combination would fall out, but no such luck.

He was about to close the Bible when he noticed red writing on the flyleaf. In big bold red letters was written: *"Look at Your Watch!"*

Julius was perplexed. He didn't know what it meant but, if his father wanted him to look at his watch, he would look at his watch. He lifted his wrist and didn't see anything special about it. *It's just a watch*, he thought.

He took the watch off to inspect it closer. He turned it over and read the inscription engraved on the back of it as he had done hundreds of times before. It read: *"To Julius. All my love, Chele"*. And under that in smaller scribe was: *"6R13L72R"*.

Julius started to laugh hysterically. He laughed so loudly that his mother actually came to the door and knocked softly. "Are you alright?" she asked.

"Yeah, Mama, I'm good!" he giggled, and waited to hear her footsteps walking away.

For as long as Julius had worn the watch, and as many times as he had looked at the inscriptions, he had never put two and two together. He always thought that the numbers on the back was a serial number. Once he looked at it again he went straight to the safe. Six right, thirteen left, seventy-two right, and the safe gave a faint click and creaked open.

Julius sat in front of the safe almost afraid to reach inside of it. He didn't know what to expect and didn't know what he would find, but he had taken the first step, and now he had to go through with it. He stuck his hand inside the safe without looking into its darkness. Reaching the back, with one swift motion he swept everything out of the safe with his left hand while he steadied himself against the safe with his right hand.

Julius' jaw dropped. There was thousands upon thousands of dollars. There were jewels as well, which were nothing that he would wear personally, but they looked expensive.

A glint of silver caught his eye, and underneath a stack of money lay a pair of chrome .45 caliber handguns with pearl handles and gold inlay. They were the prettiest guns that he had ever laid eyes on.

He spotted an old picture of his mother and father, obviously taken during a happier time. It looked as though they had taken the picture in a photo booth or at a carnival, but they were definitely having fun. His mother looked so young in the picture. She couldn't have been no more than twenty two or twenty three years old. It was funny to Julius to see his father smiling in the photo, because his father was so rough. In this picture though, he smiled, and the smile was sincere, as if in that particular moment in time there was nowhere that he would have rather been.

Julius reached for a Swisher Sweets cigar box, and when he opened it there were more pictures. There was a picture of his father and his Uncle Charlie standing side by side. Julius Sr. was holding a newborn baby with his arm around a woman that wasn't his mother. He had never seen the woman before. He turned the picture over and on the back was written: *"Taken October 19, 1967. Mommy, Daddy, Uncle Charles and Devon Gage."* Devon Gage? He didn't know anybody in his family named Devon, and his mother had never mentioned it. He was confused, but he continued to go through the contents of the safe.

He rummaged through more pictures and found a picture that looked so old that it was starting to peel and rip. It was a photo of a young, fair skinned black man that could have easily passed for white or Spanish. He was sitting next to a dark skinned woman with long, silky black hair. She bore an uncanny resemblance to his father and uncle. Her hair was braided in two long pigtails, and she looked sad in the picture. Her eyes looked tired and weary, as if from too many sleepless nights and not enough appreciation. Julius turned the picture over, and written on the back was: *"Nathaniel and Gertrude, Arkansas State Fair, 1947."* He recognized the names as his grandparents. This picture must have been taken around the time that his grandfather killed his grandmother. Julius' father had told him that his mother had been murdered by his father in 1948.

Julius pushed the picture to the side, wondering how a man could kill a woman so beautiful. By all standards she was gorgeous. Her skin was flawless, and her eyes were the color of water. To be that dark and have light colored eyes gave her a modern-day model look. Julius Sr. had told his son that his father had killed his mother because she was too pretty for him, and now Julius understood. His grandmother had striking features.

He picked the picture up again and stared at it. He couldn't see why his grandmother would be interested in his grandfather. He was a spritely man with kinky hair and fair skin. Julius thought he looked like a nappy headed white man. His hair was sandy red, and freckles all but covered his entire face.

Oh well! Julius thought. *That was a different time.*

Julius then noticed a bundle of letters that were tied together by red ribbon. They were addressed to his father, from a Michelle Quivers. None of the letters were opened, just neatly bundled and tied with the ribbon.

There was one letter that was not in the bundle, and it was also addressed to his father… or so he thought. But as he looked at it closer he noticed that it was actually addressed to *him* from his father. He tried to contain his excitement, but it was hard to do. His hands began to shake a little bit as he continued to fumble with the envelope, trying to open it. Once the envelope was open, he sat against the door of his bedroom so that his mother could not burst in, and he began to read:

My son, my seed, my heart:

If you are reading this, more than likely I am no longer with you. Hopefully you are reading this at a time when you can understand the contents of this letter.

Baby boy, there are those that will wish to see you fail. My hope is that you don't give them the satisfaction. I want you to know what you are up against. Stay away from the bad things, son. The men that are responsible for me not being here are as follows: Booty Green, Rabbit, and Yellow Shoes. They are my enemies, and my enemies are your enemies. They hate me, son, not by my own doing, but because your father refuses to be a follower.

I want you to know that I love you unconditionally, son. I always have and always will. I want to share some things with you that may or may not tarnish my memory in your mind.

In this safe you will find multiple pictures. These photos are meant to give you a sense of history concerning my side of the family. Your Uncle Charles will be able to answer any other questions that you might have concerning our family.

In the bundle of pictures you will find a picture of your brother. He is my oldest son, your brother from my loins. I never mentioned him, because in my eyes you were too young to fully understand. His mother and I never married, but he is a "Gage" just the same. He may still be in Michigan, and if he is I want you to find him. He is your link to me. He is a few years older than you. You have never met, but I made his mother promise to tell him about you, and her being a woman of her word I'm sure he knows of you.

Forgive me, son for not bringing this to you sooner, but life is often too complicated for the minds of children.

Love you always,
Daddy.

Julius finished reading the letter with mixed emotions. On the one hand he was excited about having a brother, but on the other hand he was pissed because he had been deprived of that link to his brother. He wondered whether his father had run into his Uncle Charlie in Heaven.

As Julius counted the money, his mind drifted to his mystery brother. He felt guilty for going through his father's things and not sharing with his brother. His brother had to be at least twenty, maybe older. Nevertheless, he would make it his mission to find him. If ever he needed an older brother, it was now.

Julius' mother had access to all of Booty Green's assets, so she would live comfortably, and Julius had more than enough money to support himself and Angelica while they were away at college. He would leave Sleepy in charge while he was away at school. As long as Sleepy's uncles knew that he was responsible for the day to day operation, then his connection with them would always be good.

Julius had a plan that would keep everybody he loved out of harm's way. The plan was simple: He would have his mother, Angelica, her mother and himself out of town at the time of Booty Green's murder. That way they couldn't be tied to it.

He made the necessary phone calls to set up the meeting with some of the Crips from his neighborhood. The BG's that he chose knew how to keep their mouths shut, and would love to make that money.

Graduation was right around the corner so he had to put his plan into motion. He would use graduation as an excuse for him and his mother to invite Angelica and her mother on vacation as a graduation gift for him and Jelly. While they were on their little vacation, Booty Green would be dealt with. Julius would make sure of it.

Chapter 35

Sins of My Father

Devon Gage sat in a rundown hotel room on the corner of Woodward Street in the Highland Park section of Detroit, Michigan. It was customary for the twenty-two year old young man to complete a job and return to the surroundings in which he felt most comfortable.

Devon looked around at the peeling paint flecked walls with its garage sale paintings hanging ever so slightly cocked and wondered how his life had come to such conditions. He had more money than he knew what to do with, but he wasn't happy.

His mother had passed away when he was nineteen, and his life had never been the same. He believed that she had died from a broken heart, because she had never fully recovered from the death of his father. Julius Gage, in his mother's heart of hearts, was the greatest thing since sliced bread. Although Devon thought that his father was a handsome man, he didn't understand his mother's fascination with a man that had gotten her pregnant and left. Not only did he leave, but a few years later he had fathered a child with his mother's best friend.

Starlet Bell and Najé Dunn had been inseparable during their time on the "chitlin' circuit", singing from bar to bar and lounge to lounge. According to the stories about the old days that Devon had heard, when his father and Uncle Charlie had walked into the lounge where his mother and Najé had been performing, both women were instantly attracted to Julius, but ultimately his mother had won.

Starlet was movie star gorgeous, and she knew it. There wasn't an ounce of low self-esteem in the small frame of Starlet Bell. She had paraded Julius through all of the lounges as if she had won a prize at the county fair.

Her attitude was almost insufferable for the dark skinned man, and after a short fling their relationship had fizzled out, but not before he'd left Star with a gift; his seed. After he found out that she was pregnant, Julius had come back and tried to make it work, but Starlet's pride wouldn't let her take him back. She had politely sent him packing. She still loved Julius, and the fact that he had been willing to make it work for the sake of their family had forever sealed him in her heart as a real man.

Being away from the lounge life and being pregnant with a child had given his mother a whole new outlook on life, so after giving birth to Devon she never returned to singing in the jazz clubs. With her not working at the clubs, it made Julius fair game, so it wasn't a surprise that he had taken interest in another woman. But what surprised Starlet most was the fact that it happened to be her best friend. When she had called and confronted Najé, things hadn't ended well, and both women vowed to never again speak in life.

His father had caused that split and it made Devon angry, but he had a little brother, his flesh and blood, and in all actuality Julius Gage Jr. was all he had left as far as real family was concerned.

******

One day, Devon had walked into his and his mother's small, dimly-lit two-bedroom apartment when he was fourteen years old and saw his mother sitting on the couch in the dark, and rocking back and forth. She was crying and muttering obscenities. He wasn't sure what to make of it, but he knew that something had to be wrong because she was basically a very strong woman. "What's wrong, Mama? Are you ok?" he asked her.

"They killed him, baby! They killed my Julius!" she said.

Devon was stunned. By the way that his mother had always talked about his father, he thought that he was untouchable... virtually indestructible.

His mother motioned for him to take a seat next to her. The three steps that it took the boy to make it to the over-sized couch seemed to take forever. His feet and his heart were heavy. His father would come to see the young man as often as he could, so Devon loved his father. His tears weren't as pronounced as his mother's were, but he cried internally nevertheless.

"Baby, it's okay to cry. Let it out," Starlet said.

"I'm alright, Mama. I mean, it's messed up, but I'm okay."

"Sit down. I want to tell you some things," she began slowly. "Regardless of what you think about your daddy, he loved you very much. We may not have always had it good, but he made sure we did have what we needed. Your father not being in the house with us was my fault. But him being gone forever breaks my heart. I love you, baby, and I'm sorry you have to go through this, and if I could take your pain away I would, I promise."

"I need for you to know that you have a little brother, and his name is Julius Jr. It's important to me and it was important to your father that you find him and build a relationship with him. He is your blood, and you need that link, baby. Your father sent a package for you, honey. It's in the kitchen." Starlet motioned to the kitchen with her free hand as she took a drag from her Newport cigarette with the other. She then kissed Devon on the forehead and stood up. Looking down at her son she could only shake her head as she walked out of the room, crying uncontrollably.

Devon walked into the tiny kitchen with its floral printed curtains. He walked to the window overlooking the alley behind the apartment. He looked down to see a couple of his friends from school leaning against the dumpster, hiding and smoking a joint. Any other time he would have yelled down at them to startle them just to get a kick out of it, but today was different day. His father had been killed and he was anxious to know what was in the package that he had sent.

He went to the refrigerator and took a long swig from the milk carton while he scolded himself for being a little pussy. He was actually afraid to open the package, but fear was not an option.

He sat down and looked at the big UPS box for a minute. Then he peeled the tape from the top of it and looked inside. Realizing that he would be unable to lift the contents up out of the box, he walked over to the kitchen drawer and grabbed a butcher knife. He split the box at every seam so that it exposed its contents. Inside was an immaculately polished black Smith and Wesson safe. On top of the safe was a black envelope, and emblazoned on the envelope in raised gold lettering was his name "Devon Gage". Devon opened the envelope and read it aloud:

"My dearest Devon:
11R-2L-31R

If you are reading this letter, then it means that I am no longer with you. Son, I have made mistakes in my lifetime, and one of my biggest mistakes is not spending more time with you. You are my oldest son, and there are certain things that I expect from you. One of the things that I expect is that you always respect your mother. Next, I expect for you to strive to be a good man, son. Your mistakes and downfalls will be your own, so never blame the next person for your problems.

My life has been like a movie, and I can't expect you to understand the choices that I have made, but I do ask that you respect them.

Please find you little brother, Julius. I am certain by now that your mother has told you about him, and if she hasn't then I am sure she had more than ample reason not to. If she has told you of him, find him. You are both from my seed, and I need for you two to be close; as close as your Uncle Charlie and I were. If you need any help finding him, then I am sure your Uncle Charlie or your Aunt Pearl can help you along your way.

Inside of this safe you will find certain things that will help you in your journey through life.

Again, I am sorry that I couldn't be there to tell you these things myself. At times I felt like a coward, but my choices were my own. I have always loved you, and even in death I always will.

Love Always,
Daddy."

Devon finished the letter and crumpled it in the palm of his hand. He wasn't bitter with his father, but the letter put him in a strange state of mind. He had grown up alone, often times lonely, wishing that he had a little brother or little sister to share his hopes and dreams with. His father had deprived him of that privilege, maybe for protection or maybe for selfishness, but whatever the case he had a sibling that he didn't know.

He thought of the combination that he'd seen on the letter, *11 right, 2 left, 31 right,* and used it to open the safe. With an audible "click", the door creaked open as he pulled on the handle.

From top to bottom and front to back the safe was packed with money. There were stacks and stacks of crisp one hundred dollar bills, and as if it had been cut out, there was a space in the center of the stacks. In that space were two chrome plated .45 caliber Desert Eagle pistols with pearl handles. On the handles in small diamonds were the initials "J.G." That was it; his father had left him two guns and a lot of money. Devon sucked his teeth and thought, *This nigga's on some James Bond shit!*

******

A knock at his hotel room door brought Devon's thoughts back to the present. It had been years since those thoughts had crossed his mind, but by his account his little brother should be close to eighteen, if he wasn't already. He made his way to the heavy wooden door and asked, "Who is it?"

"It's Shayla, baby! Open the door!"

Devon opened the door to reveal a tall, slender, young dark skinned girl with a curvy body. She was Devon's go-to girl for everything from guns to Chinese food. There was nothing that she couldn't get her hands on, and he loved that about the young girl.

Shayla was nineteen years old and had been on her own since age thirteen. She wasn't at all what you would expect from a girl that had been on her own since an early age. If anything, she was the exact opposite. Shayla Drake was extremely cultured, and detested whores. It had taken a while before Devon could even get to second base with her, but that challenge only served to make him love the young lady even more.

"What up, baby?" Devon asked with an obvious smile.

"I came to bank that paper, babe. You got something for me?" she asked, all business.

Shayla handled all of Devon's affairs, from the booking of his flights to the shipping of his guns. She was his personal assistant/secretary/lover/gun dealer. He was happy with her because she never got too serious on him, and he knew from the way that she talked that she wasn't everybody's pussy. He liked that a lot.

She sat down at the table that was positioned in front of the hotel room window, reached into her Chanel purse and pulled out a large bag of budded up marijuana. "You feel like smoking, Gage?" she asked.

"Yeah, no doubt, babe! Roll up!"

Shayla looked at Devon and smiled. He was a handsome man. His features were so strong that they practically overpowered his face. To her he looked like he was supposed to be darker than he actually was, but he was beautiful to her just the same.

"Paper or blunt, sweetie?" she asked. She knew that he would choose the paper because he hated the way blunts made the weed taste.

His mind was preoccupied though, and he said, "It don't really matter, baby."

To her, that statement alone said that something wasn't right with him.

She poured the green out onto the table and the strong pungent odor filled the small motel room. She pulled a small pair of scissors from her purse and began cutting the buds into small, stringy strands. After she was done, she took two Zig-Zag rolling papers, licked the adhesive and stuck the two papers together. She liked to roll really big joints, and putting the papers together made it double the regular size. She twisted the weed into a perfect joint, lit it and watched the tip glow bright orange. The smoke swirled around her head in a cloud of grey and white smoke. She took another deep toke and held in the fumes while looking at the joint as if she was in disbelief at how potent it was.

She then passed it to Devon, and when he took his first drag his mind was immediately clear. "I'ma hafta take a trip, baby, and I might need you to go with me. This ain't the normal business trip though, Ma. This is some family shit, but I need you by my side."

Devon had never asked her to go anywhere out of town with him, not on business or otherwise. She felt honored, but at the same time she was concerned. He was a very private person and he guarded his business and his emotions with stone walls and barbed wire.

"I never told you this, baby, but I got a little brother down in Texas and I need to find him," he said.

"Find him?" Shayla asked.

Her surprise was evident, but Devon didn't really feel like going into details. "All I can tell you is that me and him got the same pops, but we never met. Our old man is dead and we are all we got... well at least he is all I got... so I'm going to find him like my father wanted me to." He said.

"No doubt, baby. I'm with you no matter what. I know we don't do the serious shit, but you're the only man I have ever loved and I would die for you. I need you to know and understand that. I'm down with you through thick and thin, but all due respect, I think this is something that you need to do alone. You and your little brother need time together to bond and get to know each other. Now, when do you want me to book your flight?"

Devon just looked at Shayla in amazement. They had met just before his mother passed, and Starlet had been crazy about the girl. She had felt like Shayla was too young for Devon, but she loved her just the same. Starlet had told him on more than one occasion that the girl had an old soul. She said that when she was older, the girl would make him or someone a good wife. But Devon wasn't trying to think about marriage so he had blown his mother's statement off.

"I gotta do some calling around find out exactly where he is. Shit, the little nigga might not even want to see me, you know? So give me a few days and I'll let you know for certain."

Devon walked to the window and looked out. The streets were busy, the hustlers were peddling their wares out on the block, and the whores were moving about from car to car and turning their twenty dollar tricks by moonlight.

Devon had taken more from his father than just his strong features. Devon Gage was a killer for hire, and he was good at it. He had started out small by beating people up at school for money. Soon he had graduated to bigger and better opportunities, and now he was making at least $25,000 a hit, and he saved almost every penny he made.

He still had most of the money that his father had left for him. Plus, his mother had left him money when she died. That money on top of what he made from his "job" made him a rich young man at an early age. He didn't want for anything, and if he did, he could more than afford it. He didn't really get into material things though.

He liked his "job". He only took contracts on shady people, and he never took jobs concerning kids or women.

He wondered if his baby brother had gotten any of their father's special "talents". A lot of things were going through his head about his younger brother: *What did he look like? What was he like? Would he accept me as his brother? Shit, if he don't like me, fuck him!* he thought.

Devon's world consisted of getting money, and he was damn good at it.

He walked to the bed, laid down on his back, put both hands behind his head and stared up at the ceiling. Shayla joined him and put the stick of weed to his lips. He took a long drag and blew the smoke in her face. She giggled and playfully straddled him. She put the unlit end in Devon's mouth and the lit end into her mouth so that he could blow her a charge. It looked as if they were kissing, when in reality he was blowing her a "shotgun".

Devon took the joint from his lips and looked at the girl. "You do know that I love you, right?" he asked with a sly grin on his face.

"Yeah, I know, Gage." She knew that he loved her, but she also knew that Devon Gage, with all of the love that he had for her, was a very dangerous man.

Shayla stood up and began to undress. She pulled her tight fitting blouse over her head and unclasped her bra. Her juicy breasts were young and firm. Her chocolate nipples poked out from her breasts like two Hershey's Kisses, and her stomach was flat and toned. Her breathing had become heavy and shallow just thinking about Devon entering her. "Are you going to just lay there or are you going to help me?" she asked him lustfully.

"I'ma just lay here. I like watching your body, baby, Got-*damn*, you fine!" he said. He enjoyed watching his young lover undress. Her slender curvaceous body was enough to make the average man climax just looking at her.

She turned to dim the lights on the lamp, and Devon couldn't help but notice her firm, round ass. Even in her jeans it looked like she had small basketballs in her pants.

She wasn't a virgin by far, and she had never lied to Devon and told him that she was. She did however let him know that she had only been with a few men, and that she didn't want her body used up. It was only after months of kind words and proof-filled actions that she allowed things to go to the next level with him. And now it was like she couldn't get enough. She wiggled out of her skintight jeans to reveal red lacey bikini underwear.

Damn, her pussy is fat! I'ma eat that shit up! Devon thought. He knew he had turned her out with his tongue, and he also knew that she was equally as sprung on his dick, and he was proud of both.

Shayla stood in front of him. Even though he was fully dressed, she could see the bulge in the crotch of his jeans. She had only slept with a couple of boys before Devon, but he was definitely the best lover that she had ever had. He brought out the freak in her and she liked it. She enjoyed being able to let herself go when she was with him. He was the only man that had ever made her consider giving head. Before she met him she used to think that only whores sucked dick.

After she had gotten involved with him, he had shown her more kindness than any other man she had ever known, besides her father. Devon had politely told her that there were no rules in the bedroom when it came to them. He had even gone as far as telling her that she was free to do as she pleased. If she wanted to fuck someone else she could do that. Just make sure his business was straight and that he was taken care of.

The truth of the matter was that she didn't want to be with anybody else. He was all she needed. He took care of her body, he took care of her mind, and being in business with Devon she made plenty of money, so there was never a need to have another man around.

She kept herself busy when he was on jobs by shopping, spending time with her father and searching for new contracts for Devon.

Shayla pulled a chair up in front of the bed and began to dance for him. She moved seductively to Guy singing in the background. Her young body writhed in excitement as Aaron Hall crooned:

> "...You can have a piece of my love,
> It's waiting for you..."

Her shadow danced sexily against the dingy white walls behind her. She gyrated against the air, making love to an imaginary lover while Guy continued to sing his song of love and lust. She seductively wiggled out of her lace panties, teasing Devon as she kicked them towards him. She put one foot on the seat of the chair and began rubbing her breasts, making sure to tweak and tease her nipples. With the other hand she explored her body, letting her hand roam until it found her moist pussy. She gasped from excitement as she put her finger inside of her honey pot.

Devon couldn't take it anymore. He got up, undressed and moved swiftly up behind her. He put his hand on top of her hand to guide it inside of her.

The hardness of his manhood pressed against the small of Shayla's back. She was unaware that he had joined in because she was lost in her own ecstasy-filled world.

He took her hand from her womanhood and licked her fingers. They were wet with her juices. Her eyes popped open. She had forgotten that he was even in the room. He spun her around to face him and kissed her deeply, letting his tongue explore the inside of her mouth. With one hand he cupped her firm butt and with the other hand he let his fingers slide inside of her wet, gushy love nest. He went deep inside, then shallow, slowly then quickly. She was so wet that the anticipation was killing him. He could feel her body trembling from excitement.

He guided her body to the bed and laid her down, and kissed his way from her lips to her neck, from her neck to her bare breasts. He left a trail of wet kisses from her breasts to her navel, and finally from her navel to his destination. He cocked her legs back until they exposed her juice box and she was unable to escape. He slipped his tongue deep inside of her until she squealed with delight. Her body bucked and twisted in sexual ecstasy. She moaned and wiggled and thrust her pelvis violently at his face.

"Please, Gage! Please, put it in!" she begged.

He was more than happy to oblige, but he had a teasingly pleasurable surprise for her. He mounted the young girl and thrust his shaft deep inside of her. He pumped hard a few times and pulled it out, only to lick her pussy again.

She was lost in a sea of confusion and frustration. He would lick it and then stick it in over and over again until Shayla felt like she was going crazy.

Finally after he was sure she was ready, he entered her. He would thrust deeply, and then barely put it in, again teasing her. He was breathing heavily and enjoying the work that he was putting in. "Turn over, Ma," he told her.

Shayla did as she was told and buried her face deep into the pillow, not wanting him to hear her screams.

He pushed her shoulders into the mattress to bring her ass up higher, positioned himself behind her and entered her gently. It felt good to him, and he didn't want to come quickly, but felt his dick throbbing and pulsating and knew he was about to orgasm, so he pulled out of her and kissed down the small of her back, trying to regain his composure. He bit her on her butt and she giggled. Devon was in an extremely freaky mood, and it showed in his breathing pattern.

"Get on top, baby!" he said in a husky, passion-filled voice. He lay down on his back while his lover positioned herself on top of him. She had one hand on his chest, and with her other hand she reached down and guided his stiff muscle inside of her. Shayla arched her back as she rode him.

As Devon pumped upward to give her the full advantage of his hardness, he felt his climax building again, so he grabbed her and pulled her close to him and rolled her over so that he was on top. He pushed her knees back so that her feet rested on his chest and pushed his love muscle inside of her as deep as it would go. Again and again he slammed his rod into her wet love until they both finished in an orgasmic eruption.

He rolled off of her onto the bed, breathing like a runaway slave.

"Damn, Daddy! You be fucking my head up with your sex game!" Shayla said.

"Oh, you like that shit, huh?" he asked, knowing full well what the answer would be. He just liked to hear her say it.

"Hell yeah, Gage. You already know that shit though, so quit playin', Daddy," she said in her sweetest voice.

Devon got up from the bed, went into the bathroom and started the shower.

He came back into the room carrying a red and black book bag. He tossed the bag on the bed to Shayla. "This is the money for those three jobs I did this week. That last job in Chi-Town was a bitch. The last mark would not show his face for shit. I got me a room at the Omni Hotel directly across from his office. I guess this muthafucka was supposed to be some big wig from the FDA or sum'n. Anyway, that job by itself was worth $50,000, so in all there's $100,000 in the bag. I need you to bank $90,000, and with the other $10,000 I need you to book my flight to DFW International for one week from today, and buy me some new clothes." With that said, he walked back to the bathroom and got into the shower.

Minutes later Shayla joined him. After they both bathed, she began stroking his member until it was rock hard again. She abruptly stopped and exited the shower, giggling.

"Damn, baby! Now you know you're wrong as a muthafucka, right?" Devon said in mock anger.

"That's just a little something to keep on your mind until next time, lover!"

He got out of the shower and lay across the bed. He loved the feeling of air drying.

Shayla watched the water glistening against his hard, toned body. She dressed quietly and picked up the book bag in preparation to leave. "Baby... baby?" she called out softly, but Devon had already drifted off to sleep.

Chapter 36
Plan, Plot & Strategize

Once Booty Green was gone, Rabbit and Yellow Shoes sat at Shoes' marble and glass dining room table, sharing a joint sipping on Crown Royal straight. In the world of gangsters, sometimes the things that weren't said were the most powerful things of all. Both men were lost in their own thoughts, but both were thinking the same thing.

"Bruh, something has to be done about this nigga Green, mane," Rabbit said, breaking the uneasy silence.

Yellow Shoes nodded in agreement. His wheels were already spinning, trying to figure out how they could play it. There was only one way to deal with Booty Green, and that was to kill him. It had to be quick and brutal. There could be no chance for him to get wind of the plot, because if he did it would start an all-out war. They had to come up with something effective, and fast.

Rabbit wasn't really an idea man, but he was an enforcer.

Yellow Shoes, on the other hand, was a quick thinker, and it didn't take him long to come up with a plan. He looked up at Rabbit as if a light bulb had gone off in his head, and Rabbit smiled. He knew that Shoes had come up with the perfect plan.

Shoes jumped up, almost knocking over their drinks. "I got it, mane! We're going to kill two birds with one stone! We're gonna murder the nigga, and the little bitch ass nigga, Julius is gonna take the fall for it! We can frame this muthafucka for the murder, and that way Green is gone, and Julius might as well be dead because he's gonna spend the rest of his life in prison!" he said in a triumphant manner.

"What are we gonna do about Najé? You know that bitch is nosey, and she's gonna fight tooth and nail for her son."

Yellow Shoes knew that there was some truth to Rabbit's concerns, but he wasn't worried. "Rabbit, that ho is gonna think Julius did it too. She knows that her son is a hot head just like his fucking daddy, so by the time she hears about the shit, that little nigga will be in shit so deep that she won't be able to dig his ass out with a shovel!" Yellow Shoes said in his southern pimp accent. "We cool, baby. Just relax," he said to reassure Rabbit.

Yellow Shoes and Rabbit both stood to lose a lot if it came to light that they had participated in Julius Sr.'s murder. In order to insure complete secrecy they would have to do it themselves. It had been a very long time since either of them had gotten their hands dirty with something like this, but it had to be done.

"Well, bruh, I guess the Three Musketeers are officially done, huh?" Rabbit asked.

"Yeah, mane. It was cool but, fuck that nigga! It's either him or us!" Yellow Shoes barked. "The end of the Three Musketeers indeed!"

Chapter 37

Natural Born Killa

Devon exited United Airlines Flight 1036 in Indianapolis International airport feeling like a new man. This was his biggest job to date, and if all went well he and Shayla stood to make a cool $1,000,000. This operation would be sensitive and risky. His target was Evan Bahy, the governor of Indiana at that time. He was supposedly a crooked politician that was in bed with all of the wrong people. Devon actually didn't give a damn what the man's dirty political dealings were. His concern was that million dollar prize at the end of the rainbow.

He exited the airport and breathed in the crisp May air. A slight brisk breeze whirled through the air reminding him that he was still in the northern United States. He walked to the curb and hailed a taxi. "My man, take me to the Omni Severin Hotel," he told the cabbie.

The taxi driver didn't say a word. He simply put the car in drive and headed towards the hotel.

"Any good restaurants near the hotel?" Devon asked, hoping to engage the man in conversation to get a feel for the people in the area.

The man all but ignored him, and Devon found him rude and obnoxious, but he decided against saying anything. He didn't want to draw any more attention to himself than was absolutely necessary.

The taxi pulled up in front of the massive Omni Severin Hotel. It was situated in the center of where the governor would be speaking at various engagements throughout the next day. He was scheduled to speak at the Indiana War Memorial at 10 o'clock a.m., the Indiana Military Park at 12 o'clock p.m., and his final stop was scheduled to be Purdue University at Indianapolis. If Devon had his way, the governor would never make that last speech.

Devon entered the hotel and nodded to a young, smooth faced, dark skinned bellboy with a white rose pinned to the lapel of his uniform. Shayla had prearranged a meeting with the bellboy. Instead of Devon having to check into a hotel, she would usually have a connect in place that would have his room key ready. The money for the key would always be left in the room for the bellboy to pick up later. The bellboy having free access to move about the hotel wouldn't draw any attention. Plus, the money was good so there was never a problem.

The bellboy moved in next to Devon while he stood at a nearby payphone inside of the hotel. "Hey, b-b-bro, it's r-r-r-room s-s-s-six oh s-s-s-six," the young man stammered.

Damn! I don't know if this nigga is scared or just stuttering like a muthafucka! Devon thought to himself. He reached the elevator just as the doors were closing.

"What floor, sir?" asked the elderly elevator operator.

"Eighth floor, please," Devon responded, not wanting the man to know his exact whereabouts in the hotel. He got off on the 8th floor and walked down the stairwell to the 6th floor.

He reached room 606 and entered, and true to form like always, Shayla had his equipment waiting for him. He unlocked the metal case and eyed his M40 sniper rifle. It was his favorite gun by far. Its body was camouflaged and it was highly accurate. He had never missed a mark as long as he had been using the rifle, and tomorrow would be no different.

There was a quick knock at the door. "Who is it?" he asked. There was no answer so he went to the peep hole, and across the hall there sat a black briefcase.

He walked back to the bed and grabbed a small 9mm pistol, threw the bed covers over the gun case and went back to the door. He looked through the peephole again, and once he was satisfied that there was no one lurking in the hallway, he opened the door cautiously. He went across the hall, retrieved the briefcase and made his way back to his room. He put the deadbolt on the door and opened the case. Inside were rows of $100 bills. He sat down and counted, and then re-counted. It was exactly $500,000, half of what he was owed. As soon as his mission was complete he would receive the other half. He closed the case and pushed it under the bed, but before he went to bed he needed to make preparations.

Devon sat on the side of the bed and picked up his phone. His heart was racing a mile a minute. He was nervous as if he was a teenaged school girl. He had Shayla track down his little brother, Julius in Dallas, and had even gotten a phone number for him. He dialed the number.

"Hello," said the voice on the other end.

"Hello, may I speak with Julius, please?"

"Yeah, what's up? This is Julius. Who is this?"

It was incredible. Even at a young age his little brother sounded just like his father. "Yeah, bruh, this is Devon... your brother."

There was a long awkward pause before Julius finally spoke again. "My *what?*"

"Your brother, man. Julius was my father too," Devon said.

"Is this some kind of joke or something, man?"

"Naw, dawg. I'm the real deal. It's a long story, but the bottom line is that we had the same pops, and I really want to get to know my little brother."

"I hear you, man. It's just weird, because I literally just found out about you, and suddenly you call me. Dawg, we got so much shit to catch up on. Man, this is exactly what I need right now," Julius said.

Devon couldn't believe how well the call was going. He was sure that he would have had to convince his little brother to even have anything to do with him, but he had welcomed him with open arms. "I want to fly to Dallas and link up and kick it. Shit, we got a lot of catching up to do," Devon said.

"Yeah. Shit, let's make it happen!"

The two brothers talked late into the night, each speaking in their respective slang.

After they were done talking, Devon wasn't sure how Julius felt, but he felt closer to his little brother than he had felt to anybody since his mother died.

At the end of the conversation his little brother had said something that really touched the older Gage boy: "Devon, man, I'm glad you called, player. I'm glad you thought enough about me to call and make a connection. Hopefully you can make my graduation, bro. Shit, we're all we got!" Julius had said and had abruptly hung up the phone.

Devon checked his emotions. There would be plenty of time to boo-hoo with his little brother, but for now he had to prepare for what tomorrow would bring. Right now sleep was calling.

******

Devon woke up the next morning exhilarated and somewhat anxious. He had a lot to do before the governor's arrival.

He had the same routine whenever he was in a hotel conducting his business. First, he would have breakfast that was pre-packed by Shayla. Next, he would go through the hotel with a fine toothed comb, removing any evidence of his ever being there. That included cleaning the entire room, spraying everything that he could have touched with a mixture of bleach and furniture cleaner, removing all the sheets, blankets and pillowcases. He went as far as to take these things with him. He didn't like loose ends, because loose ends lead to prison time.

After completing his ritual, Devon put on a pair of Latex gloves and waited. He took his time and boiled water to clean and sanitize his rifle shells. He never left shells behind, but in the event that he did he didn't want any of the repercussions that could come with carelessness. He loaded his banana clip, checked his scope for accuracy and screwed the silencer into place.

Then it happened. He could see down below that something was going on. The police were speeding through the streets and positioning themselves at every corner. He was confident that he was far enough away to not have to worry about them.

The rifle that he had chosen was accurate up to one mile, and his hotel was just a little over a quarter mile so he could blow the sweat off of the governor's eyebrow and never be seen.

Black Chevy Suburban SUV's pulled up and circled the square where the governor was giving his speech. *Good Lord! They act like the damn president's finna give a speech up in this bitch!* he thought. It didn't matter to Devon. Nothing but God could save the man now. He was on a mission, and until that mission was complete he couldn't rest.

He cracked his hotel room window and the sounds of a busy morning came pouring into the room. Below, cars roared by, horns blared, and you could hear the hustle and bustle of the manic morning.

Devon wasn't concerned about the noise; he was concerned with wind conditions. He tore a small piece of paper from a tablet inside of his duffle bag and let it fly outside of his window. It flittered aimlessly to the street below, signaling to him that the wind was calm.

Devon picked up his rifle and dialed in his scope and aimed at the stage where the governor would deliver his words of wisdom and praise to the veterans that had come to hear him speak. He needed to get the job done and be gone before housekeeping came to his room. It was now or never.

The governor took the stage surrounded by bodyguards and undercover policemen. Uniformed police officers made their way through the growing crowd looking for any signs of trouble.

The governor raised his hands to silence the crowd, and a hush came over the anxious audience.

Devon's scope was dialed in, and he had the governor's temple in his crosshairs. He squeezed the trigger lightly, and the rifle spit to life. *"One shot, one kill,"* his father had told him years earlier.

The governor's lifeless body dropped to the stage floor and all hell broke loose.

Devon stood up, closed the window, threw his rifle in its case, picked up his duffel bag, took off the Latex gloves and exited the hotel room. He walked nonchalantly down the hall until he reached the elevators. Once downstairs, he made sure to look as ordinary as possible. He made it to the street and immediately hailed a cab. "What's going on out here, bruh? People are running around like they're losing their minds," he asked the cabbie in a proper voice.

"I have no idea, man. Prolly sum'n with that punk ass politician!" the cabby laughed.

Devon mumbled a very low, "Oh!" and let the conversation drift into obscurity. "To the industrial district, please," he said, giving the driver a destination.

Chapter 38

Belly of the Beast

It had been many years since Rabbit had first met Booty Green and Yellow Shoes, and for the first time since meeting the men he questioned his loyalty to the pair. He was proud of his ability to remain loyal, but the fact of the matter was that Yellow Shoes had known Booty Green a lot longer than he had known Rabbit.

Rabbit reclined in the comfort of his Italian leather seat, wondering where he stood in the scheme of things. If it was that easy for Yellow Shoes to have Booty Green murdered, then he had to be expendable too. Yellow Shoes would eliminate any and everyone that could send him back to prison. But prison wasn't an option for Rabbit either. He would also do whatever was necessary to avoid the inside of a jail cell.

The first time Rabbit met Yellow Shoes and Booty Green was inside the walls of the Coffield Prison Unit. Rabbit was only nineteen years old when he was sentenced to five years for petit larceny. He could have gotten a simple probation, but instead of his sickly grandfather coming to speak on his behalf, he crucified him in court. He had informed the judge that he had taken the boy in after both of his parents had abandoned him for the lure of drugs in the streets. He said that Rabbit was a trouble maker with sticky fingers, and that he was tired of trying to encourage the boy to do the right thing. It was emotionally and spiritually draining. He had even cried, recalling some of Rabbit's antics, and finally insisting that the strain of raising a teenager at his age was killing him, and that his grandson needed to be taught a lesson.

The judge being an old, silver haired white southerner was more than happy to oblige, sentencing the young hoodlum to the maximum amount of time allowable.

Rabbit was terrified. He had sat in the county jail for months before they sent him to Coffield...

******

"Robert Carter, hat on tight! You're on the chain!" the CO yelled.

He packed his belongings slowly and exited the county jail, shackled in leg irons and handcuffs. He was ushered onto a white bus that looked eerily similar to an oversized school bus, only it had blacked out windows with bars attached. The white transporter had the words "Texas Department of Corrections" painted in bold black letters across the side of it. The ride was long and dreadful for the young man.

Nineteen year old Robert Carter stepped off of the Bluebird bus into a world of thieves, murderers, booty bandits and hardened criminals. He was a backwoods country boy from Nacogdoches, Texas, and what he had in the way of street smarts wasn't much.

He felt his knees quivering, and as hard as he tried he couldn't seem to gain his composure. An inherent fear of being raped, beaten and sodomized magnified his ordeal to surreal heights, and it showed. The constant taunts and whistles made him even more nervous, because the leers and jeers that would generally be reserved for females were now aimed at him. "What the fuck have I gotten myself into?" he wondered aloud.

"You keep asking stupid ass questions like that and one of these turd burglars is gonna be getting in that little firm, tight booty, you got boy?" one of the old convicts sneered.

Rabbit winced from the sting of the convict's harsh words. He could tell by his look and demeanor that this was neither his first nor last time in prison. He fought the urge to exchange snide comments with the man, but his pride was hurt.

"Say, look out, sweetie!"

"Goddamn, Red!"

"Oh shit! Fresh meat!"

"I'm gettin' me some of that!"

Those were just a few of the things that Rabbit kept hearing as he walked the long outside corridor.

Twenty foot high chain linked fences with razor wire lined both sides of the bleak concrete walkway leading to the intake area. When the group of inmates including Rabbit made it to the red brick building, he was relieved to be away from the gazes of the much more experienced and institutionalized convicts.

He walked into the building not really knowing what to expect. His nervousness was very apparent, and he had gotten that tingling sensation that often times hit him when he was uncomfortable or in danger. He just dropped his head and shuffled past an obese prison guard.

There were inmates in the intake area from just about every region of Texas: Dallas, Houston, San Antonio, Austin, and everything in between. White, black and Mexican inmates congregated within the open space, oblivious to segregation or color lines.

Doing a quick scan of the room, Rabbit noticed that there had to be close to two hundred men in the intake area ready to begin their new lives as convicts. They were escorted into a large open area that resembled a gymnasium with no basketball goals; only high walls and even higher windows. The men were lined up in rows of twenty, made to strip head to toe and drop their clothes at their feet.

"First things first!" shouted an elderly CO. "My name is Captain Ferguson, and I will be addressed as such! My name is not 'man', 'boy', 'buddy' or 'hey'! We have two rules here on Coffield Unit. Number one, do as you're told. And number two, mind your own God damned business and you might make it home alive!" He continued. "First row of men, take five steps forward, bend over and spread your ass cheeks!"

Rabbit was livid. He couldn't believe it. This had to be the most humiliating display of an abuse of power that he had ever seen. Two rows in front of him were naked men, bent over at the waist and exposing their assholes for the world to see. Rabbit looked straight ahead, careful not to gaze or stare for fear that someone might think he liked what he saw. A muffled giggle drew his attention to his

236

immediate left where a man had somehow managed to get an erection from the sight of another man's exposed butt.

The CO's walked to each man, looked into his crevice and had him cough. Row by row they repeated this duty until every man had been thoroughly checked.

They were then corralled into a shower stall with hundreds of shower heads, and given a short period of time to shower. The water was excruciatingly cold, and the time that they were given to shower was barely enough time for Rabbit to wash his face, let alone his entire body.

As they left the shower they were each told to stop, spread their legs and hold out their arms. Each man was sprayed with some sort of medicine that smelled of sulfur. Rabbit later learned that it was a solution used to kill crabs in the event that you had them. They sprayed everyone with it, whether you had the parasites or not.

He was then handed a towel and directed to another room where a trustee inmate was handing out prison uniforms.

"What size you need, boy?" the trustee asked him.

"Size 30 pants, a large shirt, large boxers and size 10 shoes," Rabbit mumbled.

"Speak up, nigga! Fuck you whisperin' fo'?" the trustee said with sarcasm and contempt clearly dripping from his every word.

Rabbit repeated his order and was given the clothes. He moved to the next doorway where he was given a linen roll that included a set of towels, two sheets and a pillowcase. He was also given a pillow and a flat plastic mattress that had seen better days. After getting his items Rabbit stepped to the side and began to dress. Being naked in front of hundreds of men was most definitely not something he wanted to get used to.

"Wake up, lil' nigga and stop daydreamin'!" Rabbit heard someone say to him. "You got to go get classified in, man."

Rabbit looked back, and it was a boy maybe his age, with the gravelly voice of an old man. His eyes were lifeless and he looked removed from the situation, as if he had performed this routine more times than he cared to remember.

Over the door directly in front of him was a wood burned plaque that read: "*Nobody Owes You Shit!*" Rabbit dropped his mattress and other belongings and walked into the office.

"Name?" an old uniformed prison guard sitting at a desk asked without looking up at the young man.

"Rabbit—I mean Robert Carter," Rabbit said sheepishly.

"Which one is it, son? Rabbit or Robert?" the man asked.

"Robert, sir." Rabbit said.

The old man asked a series of questions. To Rabbit it seemed as though the man was trying to get inside of his head. He wanted to know about Rabbit's home life, whether he had any drug habits, if he had homosexual tendencies, etc. He then handed Rabbit a piece of paper with his housing location. At the bottom of the green sheet was written '1AP'.

"Where they got you at, man?" someone asked him.

Rabbit looked at the paper and said, "It says 'F Wing'." He shrugged.

"Damn bro! That's the *gladiator* wing! Them fools over there fight all the time!" the boy said.

And just like that, Rabbit's nervousness increased instantly.

A trustee pointed him in the direction of his cell block, and he walked aimlessly towards F Wing, hoping it wasn't as bad as the man had told him it was. He reached the cell block, and it was like a scene from "Alcatraz".

A CO took the paper from the young inmate, looked it over and handed it back to him with a sly smirk on his face. He unlocked the steel bars leading to the wing. The metal clanged to life, and Rabbit could hear the gears turning as the heavy bars open to reveal his new home.

Rabbit pushed a plastic cart containing his prison belongings onto the block and looked around. The cell rows were three tiers high with bars as far as the eye could see. He made his way up the stairs dragging his belongings close behind. He reached his cell, went in and placed his things on the top bunk.

A muscular white convict with countless tattoos lay in the bottom bunk eyeing Rabbit menacingly. "Don't talk to me, don't look at me, and don't touch none of my shit, boy, and we should get along just fine!" the racist warned him.

Rabbit simply ignored the man and made his bunk.

"Chow time! Chow time!" came the call over the loud speaker.

Rabbit filed out onto the run with the rest of the inmates headed towards the chow hall. He was starving. He hadn't eaten since he left the county jail hours before and he could hear his hunger. It sounded like he had a lion roaring from deep inside of his bowels.

The chow hall was a mad house. Men moved quickly from the chow line with trays that were filled by trustee inmates to long rows of stainless steel tables.

Rabbit took a seat at the table with a group of convicts from his wing.

"You lost, boy?" an old black man asked him. He looked irritated, as if Rabbit had somehow crossed into forbidden territory.

Rabbit picked up his tray ready to leave, but was stopped by another inmate. "Hold up, bruh. You ain't gotta go nowhere. This old muthafucka needs to either shut up or bump it down. Sit down and eat your food, man. You ain't got much time," the man said. He continued. "My name is Booty Green, and this here is my playa partner, Yellow Shoes."

"What's happening, my man? Like my boy said, take a seat and scarf down that chow, because it won't be long before they run us off," Yellow Shoes said.

And just as the men had said, as soon as Rabbit got deep into his food a guard walked up and knocked on the table. Every inmate at the table stood up and made their way to various trash cans to dump their scraps. Rabbit followed closely behind Yellow Shoes and Booty Green. The pair seemed cool, and he was in desperate need of friends.

They reached the cell block and took a seat in the day room. Convicts were milling about, some watching television, some involved in various games such as dominoes or chess.

"So check it out, player. You can't let these parasites see you sweat, baby boy. You have to be aggressive, because if you're not, they can smell fear and they will eat you alive," Yellow Shoes said.

"I know, man. I'm just scared, bro. I have never even seen the inside of a prison before now, so this shit is brand new to me," Rabbit said.

"Yeah, I hear you, brother, but you gotta watch your ass in here. It's a bunch of booty bandit niggas in here that would love to sample your virgin ass," Booty Green said.

Rabbit recoiled in horror. The thought of another man touching him made his stomach turn.

Booty Green noticed the frightened look on his young friend's face and said, "I'm just fucking with you, bro. As long as you stick with me and Shoes, you'll be just fine."

There was a commotion on the third tier directly in front of Rabbits cell. The three men watched as his celly, "Mr. White Muscles" was confronted by a gang of Mexicans. The argument was loud and drew all of the wrong attention. Unfortunately, the attention that they drew brought out the rest of the Mexican gangsters on the block.

"You stole my *mota, pinche'* white boy!" a Mexican named Castillo yelled.

"I ain't stole shit from you, wet back! I'm a lot of things, but a thief ain't one of them!" Mr. Muscles pleaded.

Castillo was handed a knife with blades on both ends and a handle in the middle fashioned from plastic. It was a crude looking weapon, but its intentions were evident. "Yeah, it was you, *vato!* And even it wasn't, you might as well have stolen it, because you are going to die for it!" Castillo spat.

The thought of the Mexicans gutting him was too much for the racist to fathom. With Mexicans closing in on both sides of him he decided to take his chances. He threw himself over the edge of the tier hoping to sustain minimal injuries, but things hadn't gone according to his plan. He landed with a dull thud in a seated position. He just sat there with his legs spread, as if he were about to play a game of Jacks. His eyes had popped out of his head upon impact and dangled from his head, barely attached to the muscles and ligaments. His spine had burst its way through the skin between his shoulder blades and the base of his skull.

CO's ran up to the bars, and almost immediately a loud siren began to whine. "Get down on the ground!" multiple guards ordered.

"This shit is gonna start a race war," Yellow Shoes said.

The guards entered into the cell block in full riot gear, hoping that someone disobeyed their orders just to have an excuse to use the thick wooden batons to restore control. That happened almost daily on the Coffield Unit F Wing.

******

Rabbit had managed to fly underneath the radar with the help of his friends, and he had been glad to show his loyalty year after year. He was the first of the trio to leave the prison, and by the time he had left all three men had dubbed themselves "The Three Musketeers" and had pledged undying loyalty to one another.

But now things had changed, and he wondered whether he was next on Yellow Shoe's list. He wished for a split second that things were as simple as they were in the old days when their main and only concerns were getting money and fucking pretty women.

Oh well! the man thought. *Better him than me!* Rabbit wasn't built for combat and he knew it.

242

Chapter 39

Long Time Comin'

Booty Green drove like a wild man, trying to get his thoughts together. It had been days since he'd talked to his two partners in crime, and he felt uneasy.

He had barely seen his wife for the last few days, and when he did, she didn't seem to have much to say. She had been withdrawn and distant. It crossed his mind that maybe she knew and maybe his past had caught up to him. Maybe Julius Jr. knew too, because he had been spending his nights away from home for the last week or so. That didn't sit well with Booty Green, because it was a school week. But Julius had finished all of his classes though, and Najé had said it was okay, so who was he to argue? But if you asked him, school wasn't over until the diploma was in his hand.

Booty Green smirked and thought, *Oh well! Fuck that little nigga! Where he's goin' he ain't gonna need no diploma! Dead men don't graduate!*

Booty Green couldn't wait until he got to the Bus Stop Lounge. He needed a drink so badly that he could taste it.

243

BlaccTopp

With everything that was going on, he needed to get back to his roots.

He had let his love for Najé blind him. He had also let her love knock him off of his bearings.

He was still getting money and his bank account was unbelievably fat, but he felt as though he had lost touch with the streets. People were looking at him like he had gotten soft... like he wasn't still Booty Green. He had always been a local celebrity in South Dallas, so to be looked upon as if he was a nobody was almost worse than death.

The bitches at the Bus Stop Lounge were plentiful, and they spread rumors like diseases. The broads loved Booty Green and he knew it. He played off of that love, but he hadn't acted on it lately out of respect for Najé. But if she was going to act like a little bitch, then he was going to do what he wanted to do.

Between the money from his bank accounts and the money he had stashed, Booty Green had in excess of $2,000,000. He had put everything in Najé's name to keep the police out of his business, so she knew where everything was; stash houses and the whole nine yards. He had made sure that her life was comfortable, and now he felt betrayed. Her actions were becoming more and more suspicious, but if she was going to act that way, then he was finished supporting her. *Fuck her! She could live like the rest of these broke bitches in South Dallas!* Green thought.

Booty Green was so caught up in his thoughts that he didn't notice the black BMW pull up beside him. They were both stopped at the stop sign, when a masked Rabbit jumped out of the passenger's seat of his car and gunned

Booty Green down at the corner of Pine and Colonial, not five minutes from his destination.

The last thought on Irving Green's mind was his love for Najé Dunn, and how could he have thought those bad things. As he lay there dying he silently apologized to his wife before death took him, and he slipped into the eternal darkness.

******

They had gotten the gun and bullets from Sleepy, who had assured them that Julius had handled both the gun and the ammunition so his fingerprints would be all over them.

Yellow Shoes had also called Julius at home pretending to be a school official and asked to speak with Najé. But Julius was home alone, which meant that he would have no alibi.

After they gunned Booty Green down, they left the spent shells at the scene. Rabbit also tossed the gun only a few feet away. And to add insult to injury, Yellow Shoes supplied Rabbit with a blue bandana to leave at the scene. With Julius being a known gang member, the pieces to the puzzle would fall right into place.

Chapter 40

Family Ties

Najé was excited for her youngest son. She was taking him to the airport to pick up his brother; his father's other son. It had been a long time since she had seen her son this happy and excited.

He and his brother had been talking almost every day since Devon had called him, and he couldn't be happier. Julius told his mother about their conversations, and Devon had never once uttered a harsh word about Najé. It wasn't a big secret the way she had come by Julius Sr., and although she wasn't exactly proud of it, she was happy that her pride and joy had come out of the situation.

After all of the years that had passed she still found herself in love with Julius Gage. They had their share of problems; there was no doubt about that. She had a quick tongue and a temper to match, and Julius' patience was as short as they came, so their relationship was a volatile mix to say the least. *There's no sense in crying over the past. What was done was done,* she thought.

They reached DFW Airport and pulled into the parking garage.

Julius smiled at his mother. She was still a very beautiful woman, and it was evident by the stares and attention she garnered from the older men in the terminal.

Najé exuded class and elegance. She was wearing a dark blue denim Gloria Vanderbilt body suit, red patent leather stiletto heels, and a red patent leather belt to match. She never carried a large purse, only a clutch. Her philosophy was to only carry what you needed, and in her case she only carried plastic. She very seldom carried cash because it was too bulky and too risky.

Julius laughed to himself. He looked like a tourist. He was holding a homemade sign that had the name "Devon" printed on it. Hell, he had never met his brother before so how was he supposed to know what he looked like.

Najé looked at the sign when he pulled it out and burst into hysterical laughter. "Why didn't you just ask Devon what he would be wearing, honey?" she asked him, and they both laughed.

Najé couldn't help but smile when she looked at her youngest son. He favored his father so much; or as they said in the circle, he was the spitting image of Julius Sr. He looked happy, like a kid in a toy store with a pocketful of money.

She wondered what Devon looked like. His mother had been a beautiful woman when she and Najé were young girls singing their nights away from lounge to lounge. *If Starlet got more refined with age as half as well as I did, she is still gorgeous,* she thought.

A tall muscular young man approached Najé and Julius. He had the same build as Julius Sr., and even though he was three shades lighter in skin color she could see the mixture of Julius and Starlet.

Devon walked up to the mother and son and extended his hand. "What's up, bro?" he said.

"What's up, Devon? It's good to finally meet you, bro. This is my mom, Najé."

Najé watched the young man, searching his face for any signs of malice, and she found none.

"Hello, Miss Najé. I've heard a lot about you," Devon said.

It was all true. Devon's mother had told him many things about Najé, but she had never once uttered a bad word to him about her friend.

"I was thinking that we could grab some dinner before you boys go off doing whatever it is you're going to do," Najé said happily. It was good to see the young men together. They reminded her of Julius and Charlie Boy.

"Yeah, that's fine, Mama," Julius said.

They made their way to the parking garage to Najés car. The two brothers talked all the way to the restaurant. Usually Najé would have found it annoying to hear the constant chattering, but Julius was genuinely happy. She could always tell his mood by the way he held his conversations. He was always cordial and respectful, but he usually had a somewhat monotone way of speaking that never really showed excitement. But when he was talking to someone he really wanted to talk to, you could almost hear the smile in his voice.

They arrived at Clara's Kitchen just before closing time. Miss Clara ushered the trio inside and sat them in a booth next to a window looking out onto Pine Street. Clara locked the door and turned over the worn sign from

"Open" to "Closed". The small diner was deserted, except for Miss Clara, the fry cook, Sam and the trio. Najé had called earlier that day to let Miss Clara know that they would be in shortly before closing so that they could have the small intimate surroundings that the café had to offer.

Miss Clara disappeared to the kitchen and emerged minutes later with a sheet cake. It had *"Happy Family Reunion"* written on it in royal blue icing. The icing that covered the cake was a blueberry flavored mixture of culinary delight, and Clara knew it. "Welcome to Dallas, baby! I haven't heard much about you, but your father was a very good man," Clara said to Devon.

He nodded and thanked the old lady.

Clara was old, but she had aged gracefully. Money had a way of preserving the looks of some. She was a petite elderly lady, barely five foot tall and had silver shoulder-length hair. Her skin was oddly devoid of wrinkles, and her oval shaped face housed a set off brilliant blue eyes. "I'll leave you all alone to catch up with one another," she said as she retired to her opulent kitchen.

Najé didn't know exactly how to bring Starlet into the conversation. She had so many questions about her old friend. If she was willing to talk, Najé would love to catch up with her. "Devon, so how is your mother?" she finally asked.

"Actually, Miss Najé, she passed away a few years back," Devon said somberly.

The mood was instantly transformed from happy and upbeat to melancholy.

Najé paused. She had never considered the possibility that Starlet was deceased. She had been a good and trusted friend when they were younger, and now she was gone.

Tears formed in the wells of her eyes at the thought of it. She was sad because of guilt and regret. Najé didn't regret the birth of her son, but rather the loss of the chance to patch up her relationship with Starlet. "I am so sorry to hear that, baby. That kills me inside. You never expect to lose people; especially if you haven't talked to them in years, you know? How did she die, if you don't mind me asking?"

Devon thought about it carefully. He had heard the stories about Najé, his mother and his father. "She died from natural causes, but I particularly think she died from a broken heart. When Daddy died, my Mom never got over that pain. She drank heavily and smoked continuously. It finally had gotten to the point where life was too painful to go on."

"I came home from the ball court one day, and there was a half empty bottle of scotch on the table and a cigarette still burning in her hand. She had died minutes before I came home. At first I thought she had committed suicide, but the coroner said the only thing she had in her system was booze and tobacco." He began to cry softly.

Julius listened intently. Seeing this side of his older brother gave him a new respect for the man. Here he was; big, handsome and muscular as if he had played football in college, and he wasn't afraid to show his emotions.

Devon felt relieved to talk about it with someone. He had kept his emotions bottled up for so long that he feared that he had thrown himself into his "job" in order to keep his mind occupied. He had lived his life alone since his mother died, and now he had his little brother.

"Man, I'm sorry, bro. I can't imagine what it must be like to have both of your parents gone. I mean, when Daddy died it messed me up for a long time, but I'm here to tell you that I got you, playa. We can share my Mama," Julius offered sincerely.

"I appreciate that, little brother, straight up. But enough about death and dying. This is supposed to be a celebration. We're not only celebrating us finding each other, but you're getting ready to graduate, little man!" Devon said.

"Yeah, buddy! I can't wait!" Julius exclaimed.

"We had better order before Miss Clara puts us out of here," Najé said. She was happy that Devon wasn't bitter, and that he was willing to embrace his little brother.

"Dog, I ain't even gonna front. I don't know how long it's been since you had some home cooking, but Miss Clara goes extremely hard," Julius said.

"It's been a hot minute, so I'm down with that!" Devon said with a smile.

They dined on ox tails, fresh collard greens, baked macaroni and cheese, drank sweet tea, and had Miss Clara's world famous sweet hot water corn bread.

Devon looked from his brother to his newly adopted mother and smiled. This wasn't Detroit, but it was now home. Life was good.

Chapter 41

Don't Hate, Congratulate

Julius was excited, but his excitement was bittersweet. Tomorrow he would be walking across the stage getting his high school diploma, but he wished his father was there to see it. But shit is the way that it's supposed to be, he reasoned. At least Devon was there to represent for his father. It was almost as good, but not quite.

Julius was beside himself with happiness also, because Booty Green had been killed. Somebody had gotten to him before Julius had gotten him. He didn't care, as long as the nigga was dead. He chuckled inside at the thought of Booty Green begging for his life like a bitch. In his mind, he felt like, *Fuck it! Everything happens for a reason, and karma is a bitch!* Booty Green had done so much dirt in his lifetime that it was bound to catch up with him sooner or later. Julius almost allowed sympathy to overtake him, but as quickly as it came, he just as quickly dismissed it. He had killed his father, so he had gotten exactly what he deserved in Julius' eyes. "Fuck that shiesty ass nigga! If he wasn't so shady his bitch ass might still be alive!" Julius said

He knew that it was hurting his mother, and even though he didn't like Green for what he had done to his father, he still hated to see his mother in pain. She was angry at Booty Green for betraying her, for lying to her, and for leaving her before she had gotten a chance to confront him, and for him dying so abruptly. But he was still her husband and she loved him. She went as far as to ask Julius if he had done it. The same tone of voice that she had used was the same tone that she used with him when Shy had been killed. It was more concern than anything. She didn't want to see her son in anymore trouble if she could help it.

Julius had reassured his mother that he didn't have anything to do with it, and that nobody that he personally knew was involved.

The detectives had come and talked to Najé earlier and asked if she would be willing to come downtown to make a statement. She had agreed, but both Najé and Julius knew what that meant. Even though the detectives weren't coming right out and saying it, they looked at Najé as a person of interest. They had questions concerning Booty Green's death because of the amount of money that Najé stood to gain. People have killed and have been killed for a lot less... a whole lot less.

Between Booty Green's bank accounts and the $500,000 life insurance policy that Najé had taken out on her husband, she was looking at upwards of $2,000,000.

The stash house money the police didn't know about, so she wasn't worried about that. Najé had collected all of the stash house money, and it totaled a little over $800,000.

At first she was angry with Green that he had withheld the fact that he had so much money put away, but she was glad that he had. Besides, she hadn't told him about the life insurance policy either, so no harm, no foul. That money along with the rest put the total close to the $3,000,000 mark. She really didn't care about that. She just wanted to make sure that Julius' college was taken care of. She had stayed on him all through high school, and now she had four years of college to help him finish. If she could do that she would be satisfied.

Julius wanted to take the three women in his life out for dinner. He had spared no expense for the night. He rented a Limo from Mr. Barrera's company, and had it stocked with Dom Perignon champagne. He knew that Dom was Mrs. Gray's favorite.

He made reservations at Najé and Angelica's favorite restaurant, Pappadeaux. It was a nice restaurant, and he always got a kick out of listening to Angelica order her food. He had taken her there for the first time on Valentine's Day and she had loved it. She spoke in the most proper manner when ordering: "Yes, I'll have the calamari, please," she had said, sounding like a Valley girl.

Julius laughed at the memory because Angelica hadn't known that calamari was squid, and the look on her face when she bit into it was priceless, and Julius had almost rolled on the floor, laughing.

Jelly was so innocent and so trusting. She had spit the calamari out into a white linen napkin. She was obviously embarrassed and leaned towards Julius and asked if she could order something else. Julius had only smiled and told her to order whatever she wanted. He had kissed her lips and told her that today was a day for lovers, and that today was her day.

Now they were about to graduate, and Julius wanted to make it special. Their mothers already knew that they planned to attend college in Atlanta, so now was the perfect time to tell them that they intended to live together.

Julius had instructed the Limo driver to pick him up at the Ambassador Hotel.

He and Devon had been downtown all morning shopping, and Julius had settled on an off white linen suit and a sand colored shirt. He chose a pair of caramel brown Cole Haan slippers and belt to match to complete his outfit. He wanted to be sharp tonight.

Devon's taste in clothing was exquisite. He was the dark to Julius' light. He picked out a grey Italian cut suit, a black silk shirt and black natural leather loafers. To Julius he looked like a member of the Mafia. *This nigga damn near dresses better than me... almost!* he thought.

His mother would already be at Angelica's house, so they would leave from there.

Chapter 42

Forever My Lady

Najé was being kind of mushy and clingy, but Julius didn't mind. That was just her way of showing how proud she was. And she had really taken to his brother.

When Julius and Devon pulled up in front of Jelly's house in the Limousine, Najé and Mrs. Gray were standing outside smoking a cigarette while waiting for his arrival. Angelica was standing outside but off to the side. She couldn't stand the smell of cigarettes. She hated that her mother smoked, and now she was stuck with two people smoking.

When Julius stepped out of the Limo all three ladies' jaws dropped. They had never seen Julius dressed like he was. Angelica ran to him, threw her arms around his neck and kissed him on the lips softly.

"Hey, baby! Happy to see me?" he asked with a smirk.

"Of course, Daddy! Damn, you look sexy! I feel underdressed!" she said.

In fact, she looked gorgeous in her spaghetti strapped sun dress with earthy colors. Her wedge heels were off-white, and her finger and toenails had been done in a French manicure and pedicure. Julius loved when she went to the nail shop because it made her look so sexy and classy.

"Naw, baby, you look good as hell!" he said. "I'd like to introduce you to my brother, Devon," he added.

"Pleased to finally meet you, sis-in-law," Devon said.

"Likewise." Angelica had talked briefly with Julius about his brother, but he hadn't gone into details. What she did know was that he was very anxious to meet his brother, and it made her happy to see him so upbeat.

Mrs. Gray and Najé walked over to the young couple, and each woman hugged Julius.

"Julius, you look like you could be my son-in-law. You're looking pretty dapper there, young man," Mrs. Gray said.

Julius just smiled and said, "That's the plan one of these days, Mrs. Gray. By the way, this is my brother, Devon."

"Hello, Mrs. Gray. It's a pleasure to meet you. Is there a Mr. Gray?" Devon asked flirtatiously.

"Maybe soon!" she replied, eyeing the young man seductively.

"Devon, we just met and you're too young to be my step-daddy, so stop flirting with my mom!" Angelica said with a smile.

They all laughed.

Julius held the door to the Limousine open for the women to enter. The ride to the restaurant was interesting to say the least.

Angelica had never been in a Limousine under happy circumstances. The only other time she had been in one was when her grandfather died.

Julius was feeling on top of the world. He had his brother there, and to see his mother, Mrs. Gray and Angelica in such high spirits made him feel good.

The three women joked and giggled while they sipped on champagne. Angelica was still nursing the same glass when Najé and Mrs. Gray were popping the cork on a second bottle of Dom.

"I just want to say this is a dream come true, Ju man. Angelica is gorgeous, bro. She reminds me a lot of my little boo in Detroit named Shayla." Devon couldn't stop thinking about Shayla. She was always in his corner no matter what the situation was.

The last hit he had done in Indianapolis had gone off without a hitch. After the hit he had gone to the industrial district and dropped the guns off where Shayla had pre-arranged to have them shipped back to Detroit, under the radar. If he was going to relocate to Dallas, then he most definitely wanted her with him.

"Thank you, bro. Shayla, huh? You need to bring her down here. I mean Jelly and I are going to college in Atlanta in the fall, but Atlanta is closer to Dallas than Detroit."

When the Limo arrived at Pappadeaux, Mrs. Gray and Najé were feeling pretty good—not drunk, but definitely not sober.

They were lead to a table in a private room in the restaurant that Julius had prearranged, but he was still able to see the entire scope of the place. Growing up the way he had, he was always extra careful, almost to the point of paranoia. He never sat with his back to an open area, ever.

He had another bottle of Dom delivered to the table, and after everybody's glasses were filled he stood up and said, "I'd like to propose a toast. First, to my Mom for pushing me through high school and always staying by my side."

"Second, to my beautiful Angelica. Baby, I have loved you since third grade. You're my everything, and I love you."

"Mrs. Gray, cheers to you for giving birth to my angel."

"Third, I'd like to say I'm happy that my brother is here to see me graduate. I love you, bro!"

"And last but not least, a toast to my father. I wish you were here, Daddy, straight up."

"Jelly, we made it baby!" he said excitedly."

They all raised their glasses to toast.

Mrs. Gray then got up to speak. "Julius, I want you to know that I used to think that you were a hoodlum and I never wanted you around Angelica. But after years of getting to know you, I know that there is nobody else that could love Angelica the way you do."

"Thank you, Mrs. Gray," Julius said modestly.

Angelica stood up next. She was smiling with tears streaming down her cheeks. She was beautiful and her face was glowing. "Baby, thank you for always being so wonderful to me. You've been the perfect gentleman since day one. Thank you. And yes, baby, we made it! Mommy, Mrs. Green, Devon, Julius, baby, I want you all to know that I love you all very much; each one of you. Devon, I know we just met, but I love you too because you have truly brought and immeasurable amount of happiness to my Julius."

She continued. "Now, I have an announcement of my own to make. Julius, baby, you are going to be a father and you two ladies are going to be grandmothers!"

Suddenly silence filled the room, and everyone seemed to freeze in place. It was a disturbing and uneasy silence that everyone at the table was well aware of. The women were watching and waiting for a reaction from Julius.

Julius didn't know how to react. His head was spinning, and he was experiencing mixed emotions. On the one hand he was happy, but there were so many questions to be answered: *Would he be a good father? Would it be a boy?* These were just some of them.

On the other hand, uncertainty set in a little bit. Julius knew that his lifestyle was foul and the last thing that he wanted to do was endanger the people he loved the most.

He moved closer to Angelica, took her into his arms and looked deeply into her eyes. Angelica didn't know whether he was looking at her or trying to look through her. "Jelly, you know I love you and having this baby will only bring us closer together. We're still going with our original plans, and I hope you're still going to college," he said.

"Yes, Julius, I want us to still do everything we planned on doing; the apartment, college, the whole nine yards," Angelica said and blushed.

"Hot damn! This is crazy! I'm gaining all kinds of family and I love it! I went from just Shayla and me to a brother, a mom, a sister-in-law, a sister-in-law's sexy mother, and now a nephew or niece!" Devon said with a smile and winked at Mrs. Gray.

Najé and Mrs. Gray just looked at one another. It was obvious that their babies were no longer babies. They had made plans without consulting either parent, asserting their independence. Life was about to change for the two teens in more ways than one. Tomorrow they were graduating from high school, and the next step was adulthood. This was not the way Mrs. Gray thought that she would get her first grandchild, but she reasoned that at least Angelica had waited until she graduated.

Najé sat there thinking that even if her youngest son was barely old enough to vote, she was still proud of him. In South Dallas, the young men were becoming statistics almost overnight. Her son had made it through so many obstacles in his young life already that she was overwhelmed with pride. A baby would set him back, but if he was excited, then she was excited for him. If he liked it, she would love it.

The group at the table had no idea just how much their lives were about to change… forever.

Chapter 43
This Shit Won't Stick

The detectives were certain that they had enough evidence to charge Julius Gage. They had fingerprints, they had the murder weapon, and an eyewitness that had called in anonymously and put Julius on the murder scene.

The lead detective had a hard-on for this case. He remembered years earlier when he'd just made detective, he had run across two gangsters named Julius Gage and his brother Charlie Gage. They had been a thorn in his side, and before he could bust them they had both turned up dead. It might have sounded heartless, but he wished that they were both alive so that he could send them to prison. This couldn't be a coincidence; *another* Julius Gage? He had no doubt in his mind that this was his son, and Detective Sweeney would make the son pay for the sins of his father.

Detective McVey was Sweeney's partner. He was a fresh faced young detective, and he didn't really understand his partner's obsession with the case. In homicide they arrested young gang bangers and hoodlums every day, but Sweeney seemed overly obsessed with this young banger. "Sweeney, why are you so obsessed with this piece of gang trash?" McVey asked him.

"My young friend, I had been working this Gage family for a long time. They had a grip on South Dallas that few people knew about. And just when I had enough evidence to bust their asses, they were both killed back to back. This little nigger will not escape prosecution!" Sweeney spat.

"Okay! Okay! Calm down!" McVey laughed.

He always got a kick out of his partner's blatant bigotry. They were both part of the "good ol' boys" network, and they used it to their advantage every chance that they got. The young detective didn't agree with a lot of his partner's ways, but he had been with the Dallas Police Department for twenty five years and had seen a lot more than McVey had hoped to see in his short career on the police force, so who was he to question his partner?

The two detectives made their way to a conference room filled with the Dallas Police Department's finest. The tactical squad, plain clothes cops and uniformed cops were all assembled, waiting for a briefing from Detectives Sweeney and McVey.

"I will make this shit brief. We are serving a high risk warrant on a very dangerous young man." He turned to a poster-sized picture of Julius that was attached to the dry erase board behind him. "This little piece of shit has money up the ass. He's a member of the 357um Gangster Crips, and he's wanted for murder. He's always armed and dangerous, which is why we're taking the precautions that we're taking," Sweeney said.

"We want to catch him away from home, totally out of his element. That decreases the chance of violence. Be careful and be mindful of your surroundings. There is no telling who will be in attendance to give aid to this bastard, so watch your asses!" McVey warned.

Detective Sweeney stared at his young partner. He wanted to bring him into his situation, but if he wasn't with the plan it could spell disaster for the seasoned veteran. They had a lot to gain and a lot to lose, but one thing for certain was that he had a considerable amount of trust for his colleague. "McVey, I need to speak with you briefly before we execute this warrant."

McVey searched his partner's face for any hint as to what could be so urgent. He credited himself for being able to read body language and faces, but he saw no signs in his. "Go ahead, Sweeney. I'm all ears."

"You asked me earlier why I wanted this young man so badly, correct?"

"Yeah, that's right."

"Well, what I told you was the truth, but I left out one minor detail. The fact of the matter is that if we can put this bastard away, we stand to make a shit load of money."

"What are you saying? He's innocent?"

"Hell no he's not innocent! Hell, he may not have committed this crime, but the crimes he has committed far outweigh the murder of some common street nigger!" Sweeney said with a sneer.

McVey didn't know what to think. He didn't like drug dealers or street people. For that matter, he didn't like black people period. But, he had reservations about sending an innocent man to prison. He was also aware that his partner could make or break his virgin career. "I'm with you,

Sweeney. Just promise me that all of our bases are covered and you'll have my back financially," McVey said.

"No worries, young man. I can promise you that this is an open and shut case. The money is as good as in the bank," Sweeney said, relieved that his young protégé had agreed to his plan.

******

Julius was nervous. He didn't like crowds. There were so many people gathered in the Dallas Convention Center that it made him paranoid. He felt like everybody was watching him.

"Why are you so nervous, baby?" Angelica asked.

"I don't know, baby girl. I just got this eerie feeling," Julius said sadly.

"Relax, baby, and cheer up. Everything will be fine, and I'm nervous too!" Angelica said, and kissed him on the cheek.

But he just couldn't shake the feeling. He thought to himself, *I should be happy as fuck.* "Fuck! This should be one of the happiest days of my life, and I'm paranoid like a dope fiend tweaking and shit!" Julius laughed. He shrugged it off as just being the jitters.

******

Devon could smell the police. They didn't smell like the average hustler, and they damn sure didn't smell like school kids. They had a distinctive smell, like they all shopped at Cheap Cologne Depot. He almost panicked when he saw them start to file in, but it crossed his mind that maybe this is what was needed because most of the teenaged boys graduating today were gang members. But he still had a funny feeling.

Julius looked back at him from his seat, and they locked eyes. It was in his face too. Devon recognized that look for certain. It was dread.

******

The ceremony was beginning, and Sweeney had taken his position along with McVey on stage. They had everybody in place, ready and waiting for the signal. The detectives were getting antsy. They watched young Julius as he walked down the aisle. Sweeney couldn't wait to put the little fucker behind bars.

The graduates' names were being called alphabetically and they were just on the D's. "...Jason Davidson; Nina Dermott; Louis Dylan..." the principal went on and on.

Sweeney had made eye contact with Julius' girlfriend, Angelica Gray as she walked down the isle. *She's a gorgeous girl... way too gorgeous for Julius Gage,* the detective thought.

Julius sat in a crowd of his peers waiting anxiously for his name to be called. If it had been left up to him, the school could've just sent his diploma to his mother's house in the mail. But he wouldn't deprive her of seeing him walk across that stage.

Ever since he started selling drugs he had never made a major purchase, but for graduation he was buying a new car for himself and a new car for Angelica. His mother thought that the money for the cars was from the trust fund that his father had set up for him, so he wasn't worried about her getting suspicious. She knew that he got his hands dirty, but she had no idea to what extent.

Julius figured that he and Angelica would go car shopping after they left graduation. His mother had planned a little get together, but they wouldn't stay the entire time. Besides, not wanting people fawning over him, he also wanted time to bond with his brother before he went back to Detroit.

Julius' family had come in from all over the United States. Family had flown in from Benton Harbor, Michigan, Belle Glade, Florida, and Atlanta, Georgia. He most definitely had family in the building.

"...Damon Edwards; Ray Elliot; Julius Gage..." the principal called out.

There it was. His name was finally called. Julius rose and began to make his way towards the stage. He could hear his mother, aunts, cousins and siblings cheering and screaming his name.

As he got to center stage he looked out over the crowd and noticed that every doorway in the auditorium seemed to be guarded not by the regular security guards, but by policemen, S.W.A.T. and tactical police. Julius dismissed it, because after all this was Lincoln High School, so anything could happen.

Julius crossed the stage with a huge smile and feeling good. He could hear his mother's words of praise. As he reached out to grab his diploma and shake the hand of the presenter, the arena erupted into wild cheers and applause.

It went deathly silent just as quickly as it had erupted once the people in the auditorium realized that the presenter had put handcuffs on the young man as he reached out to take his diploma.

Julius was angry and dumbfounded, but he didn't resist. As Detective Sweeney was slapping the cuffs on him, the tactical squad was making their way down the aisles with weapons drawn, so he knew that there was no need to run because there was nowhere to go. Julius felt numb. He had no idea what was going on. *If these bitches think I'm lying down for a dope charge, they are crazy as fuck! I'll be out of this muthafucka by morning!* he thought.

As Detective Sweeney led Julius away from the stage, the old white detective began to smile a sinister smile. Julius could smell the scent of stale cigarette smoke and last night's vodka. Sweeney smelled like a common street bum, and on his teeth you could see the stains from too many years of cigarettes and cheap coffee. He didn't look at all like what Julius' idea of a detective was.

Sweeney noticed the young man looking at him with contempt, and his smile broadened, "Yeah, I got you, nigger! You're going away forever! Nigger, as long as Maxwell House makes coffee you will be in prison! Fuck the Gage family! Do yourself a favor and kill yourself, boy. Go and join your no good daddy and your uncle. And when you get there, tell 'em Rabbit and Yellow Shoes send their regards!" he spat.

BlaccStarr Media Group

P.O. Box 9451
Port St. Lucie, FL 34985-9451

Order Form

Name: _____

Address: _____

City: _____ State: _____ Zip: _____

Qty	Title	Price	Total
	The Hustle Chronicles	$15.00	
	-Coming Soon-		
	The Hustle Chronicles 2	$15.00	
	Tainted	$15.00	
		Subtotal	
	...Shipping charges...	**Shipping**	
	Media Mail First Book........ $3.95	**Total**	$_____
	Each additional book...........$1.50		

No Personal Checks Accepted
Make Institutional Checks or Money Order payable to:
BlaccStarr Media Group

BlaccStarr Media Group

P.O. Box 9451
Port St. Lucie, FL 34985-9451

Order Form

Name: _____

Address: _____

City: _____ **State:** _____ **Zip:** _____

Qty	Title	Price	Total
	The Hustle Chronicles	$15.00	
	-Coming Soon-		
	The Hustle Chronicles 2 **(2-14-13)**	$15.00	
	Tainted	$15.00	
		Subtotal	
	...Shipping charges...	**Shipping**	
	Media Mail First Book........ $3.95	**Total**	$_____
	Each additional book..........$1.50		

No Personal Checks Accepted
Make Institutional Checks or Money Order payable to:
BlaccStarr Media Group